Double the Risk

by

Samantha Cayto

Book Two
Boston's Brave

Double the Risk

Contact Information: info@thewildrosepress.com

Cover Art by *Diana Carlile*

The Wild Rose Press, Inc.
PO Box 708
Adams Basin, NY 14410-0708

Visit us at www.thewilderroses.com

Publishing History
First Scarlet Rose Edition, 2014
Print ISBN 978-1-62830-699-6
Digital ISBN 978-1-62830-700-9

Published in the United States of America

Choosing between them will be impossible…

"Shall we go?" He held out his hand, as if to usher her to his side. When she hesitated, his smile dimmed. "Is something wrong?"

Cassidy wet her lips and noticed how Ronan's gaze followed the movement. "I need to tell you something before we leave. It might change your mind about tonight."

"I doubt it, but please go ahead."

"I went out with Diego last night. It was a spur of the moment thing, and…"

"I know. He told me this morning."

"He did? What exactly did he tell you?"

"That he'd dropped by on the chance that you were free and asked you out to dinner."

"Oh. Um, okay. Was that it?" Jesus, what was she asking him? Did she really want to know if Diego bragged about having sex with her? Besides, while she didn't know him well, she couldn't believe Diego was the fuck and tell kind of guy.

"That was it." Ronan frowned slightly. "He didn't give me details, and I didn't ask for any. It's none of my business what you two did last night."

Well, that was awfully mature of him. It flew in the face of everything she thought she knew about men. "Then it doesn't bother you?"

"The only thing that would bother me is if you're only going out with me tonight because you're too polite to cancel."

"Oh! No," she was quick to assure him. "I want to go out with you." She felt her cheeks heat up and had to fight to keep from cupping them with her hands. She was so not good at this femme fatale stuff.

Ronan's megawatt smile was back. "Great, let's go."

Dedication

To my cousin, Sean,
an Irish cop in the best Boston tradition.

Prologue

"What are you going to do, Rory?" The fear in his mother's voice was obvious to Ronan.

"Sheila, my love, don't worry about it." His father tried to put his arms around her, a look on his face he only wore when he was about to cajole his wife of more than twenty years.

His mother deftly avoided the hug and moved to the other side of the kitchen. "Don't tell me not to worry when I can see as plain as day how much *you* are."

His father sighed heavily and ran his fingers through the head of black hair still thick in his middle-age. "I'm not so much worried as pissed, honestly. I thought better of these men. Hell, I went through the academy with some of them. I thought they were good cops, honest ones. They're tarnishing the badge," he added, his voice lifting.

His mother glanced around. "Lower your voice, Rory," she admonished. "Finn will be home any time now, and Ronan is coming for dinner. I don't want them to hear any of this."

Ronan was already home, lacrosse practice having ended early when Bobby McCoy broke his leg. That's what he got for showing off, not that Ronan would ever say as much out loud. Standing quietly in the hall, he listened to his parents talking, understanding quickly that something was up. He'd seen the tension in his

1

father these last few months every time he came home from college looking for a better meal than they offered up on campus. Perhaps now, he'd understand why.

"Neither do I," his father said in a quieter voice. "I've told them all their lives that being a Boston cop was the best job in the world. I hate to have to tell them there are worms eating at its core."

"It's not your fight, or at least not entirely," his mother amended quickly when his father scowled at her. "Please don't take this on yourself anymore. You need to tell others. You need to tell James."

His father's scowl deepened. "I don't want to go to James until I have more proof and know who all is involved. He's up for promotion again, and you know he's going places, Sheila. I don't want to put him in a bad spot."

"You do him a disservice by keeping him in the dark. He's as good a cop as you and would want to know the truth."

Running his hand down his face, his father said, "Maybe you're right. I'll bring him into the loop soon, I promise." He opened his arms. "Sweetheart, I don't want you to worry, though. I'm being careful, and I know what I'm doing. I promise."

"Oh, Rory." His mother walked into his father's arms and hugged him tight. "I can't stop worrying about you. You know that."

As his parents stood wrapped in each other's arms, Ronan stayed still so as not to disturb them. But his mind whirled with what he'd heard. Something bad was going on, and his father was in the thick of it. Whatever it was, it had his mother worried, and now he was worried, too.

Chapter One

The City of Boston clung tenaciously to summer, hot and humid already at six in the morning. It was going to be a scorcher, hitting near ninety, and as early as it was, the sweat had dripped off Ronan Callaghan before he'd gone more than a block. That was New England weather. It could be as cold as Montana and as steamy as Florida. Given that it was early September, the heat and humidity weren't a complete surprise.

Ronan didn't care or even notice that his T-shirt was plastered to his torso as he turned into the last block of his morning run. The college students were back in class so he wasn't the only one huffing his way down the sidewalk. He didn't mind that, either. When he'd finally moved out of the family home for good, he'd deliberately picked the Brighton area to be near his alma mater, Boston College, and its student body.

After his parents' murder, he'd been forced to return home and commute, having tasted college living for only one semester. That's what he got for deferring college until January. Someone had to look out for his kid brother, Finn, and with his older brother, Daire, working full time as a new cop, that someone had been Ronan.

He hadn't minded, not really. He'd done it without even being asked. Sure, a fourteen-year-old boy was a major pain in anyone's ass. One who was also mourning the brutal loss of his parents, even more so. It had been tough keeping tabs on the kid, making sure he got to school on time, did his homework, and cleaned his room, everything Ronan had loathed to do himself at that age and older. All this was while dealing with his own grief and anger and trying to adjust to being a college student and young adult with the angst that entailed. There hadn't been time anymore to go to parties or just hang out with other students after class. There was laundry to do and dinner to fix. The weekends had been filled with house cleaning and food shopping.

Yeah, Ronan had become the "mom" of the house, filling his mother's shoes to the best of his ability and always feeling as if he'd fallen short. One day he'd been lecturing Finn about missing dinner and not calling, and suddenly he wondered when in the holy hell he'd grown his mother's forefinger. The one she'd shaken countless times in front of his face. Still, he'd done it all because he was a Callaghan and Callaghans always took care of their own.

Those days were past him. He'd graduated from college and the police academy. He wasn't merely a cop but a detective, and knowing he followed his brother up the ranks, the way Callaghans had always done, filled him with pride. Finn didn't need him anymore, hadn't for years really. Finn had put on the badge months ago, and even had an undercover assignment under his belt, plumping up his file. And his brother was making a home of his own, living with another cop and raising a teenage boy to boot.

Just the thought made Ronan grin. Every time Finn bitched about the pain-in-the-assedness of teenagers,

Ronan told him to talk to the hand. Been there, done that, bro, and welcome to the club. Finn's partner, Michael, was a good guy, so Ronan didn't worry about Finn anymore. Sure, he still had bad dreams about the night they'd almost been too late finding Finn during the undercover job. He'd wake up in a cold sweat with visions of Finn's naked and bloody body in the grip of the leader of the pedophile ring they busted. On those days, it was doubly great to slip on his ratty clothes and hit the pavement.

Maybe it was kind of pathetic that he wanted to immerse himself in the community he'd missed out on as a student. He didn't care. It wasn't as if he was hanging out at frat parties or anything. He just liked the vibrancy of the location, and it wasn't as if at the age of twenty-six, he was some lecherous aging guy ogling the co-eds. He wasn't even into his age group. He liked slightly older women, seasoned ones who knew what they were doing and not necessarily looking for forever. Having spent much of his young adulthood being too much of an adult, he liked to play it easy and loose.

Ronan pushed his speed because he needed to burn off the stress already building within him. Normally, he loved his job and couldn't wait to get the day started. This one, however, could turn out to be a bitch. He was getting a new partner. He'd known it was going to happen as soon as Vicki told him she was pregnant. Only four months into her pregnancy, and she'd been put on bed rest. Twins, Christ Jesus. She and her husband would have their hands full. He couldn't begrudge her the need, of course, but they'd been partners for less than a year. As the older, more experienced detective, she'd been his mentor. Her steady and methodical manner had worked wonders at curbing his impulsiveness. Now, who knew what kind of cop he'd be paired with? He couldn't even think of anyone in the department that was currently solo. Maybe they'd give him a rookie detective. Then he'd be the senior man, and he wasn't so sure he was ready for that.

Shit, he'd rather have the twins. He'd rather be the one to *give birth* to the twins.

As his feet pounded the pavement and the sweat dripped into his eyes, he willed his mind to shut off. Worrying about things never helped. He'd just have to wait and see. He put in a burst of speed as he ran up the front stoop of the duplex he rented. A nice cool shower before heading into work would slap him more awake. Iced coffee on the way to the station was also a must. He needed to be on his toes today in particular.

Throwing himself into the shower stall, he leaned into the stream and sighed with the pleasure of it. His cock sprang up, much like Pavlov's dog. Living on his own meant he could spend as much time in the bathroom as he wanted and jerk off whenever he felt the urge. His morning showers had turned into play time given the dry spell he was going through date-wise. He pumped some body wash into his palm and clasped his dick. He teased himself with long, slow strokes that made him groan. With his other hand, he rolled his balls. The rhythm his hands danced to was automatic. He knew just how to coax his pleasure to climb at a steady pace.

No hurry, no one else to please or worry about. Just him squeezing his cock on the upstroke and sliding his thumb through his slit. He tugged his sack away from his body, grunting at the small bite of pain. They tightened in his grip, signaling his climax was near. He picked up the pace, jerking his dick hard and fast. As the first rope of cum shot out, he clasped more firmly with both hands and pulled himself through the orgasm. He gasped into the spray, choking on the water entering his mouth. When his knees threatened to buckle, he released his balls and braced his palm against the wall.

He stood panting for long minutes, until his brain kicked back into gear. He needed to get going so that he could meet his new partner. Now that he was a relaxed as he was ever going to get, it shouldn't be too bad. How much of a douche could his new partner be?

****

Diego Nieves parked his Harley in the precinct employee parking lot and debated whether he needed to bring his helmet in with him. Then he remembered the chance of being arrested never stopped anyone from committing a crime, and he tucked it under his arm. Man, Boston was as steamy as New York this time of year. Somehow, he expected it to be cooler because it was a little farther north and Boston Harbor wasn't as far inland as New York's, at least it seemed that way to him. Whatever, it was fucking ninety degrees with seventy percent humidity. He'd taken the risk of wearing just his suit on the bike and no leathers. If he'd gone down, the doctors would have been piecing his skin back in strips. Fortunately he was used to riding in the City, the real one. Boston drivers had nothing he hadn't seen before.

He entered the building and was grateful to get a blast of cool air. He flashed his credentials to the desk sergeant, a badge so shiny new it practically blinded him. The guy, an older man whose face was probably as red as it was all year round, gave it a quick look before buzzing him through. Diego nodded in thanks, a brief smile on his lips. He wanted this to be a good transfer, smooth, a new start. He was ready for it. Whether Boston was ready for a new cop, and a Puerto Rican one at that, remained to be seen.

If you ain't Irish, you're nothing up there.

His former partner, Julio, had been adamant about that, although he'd been keen on Diego staying in New York, so what he said had to be taken with a grain of salt. It seemed too nineteenth century to believe the Irish had a lock on the Boston police force. On the other hand, a lot of the name badges he saw as he walked down the halls of the precinct sounded Irish enough. He'd also wrangled the name of his new partner out of the lieutenant, and damned if it wasn't a guy named Callaghan. Ronan Callaghan. Of course he'd done an Internet search on the guy. Pure Boston cop royalty with a murdered father in the mix. He really hoped he was wrong, but his gut told him his new partner wasn't going to be to his liking.

His mother would say he was borrowing trouble. He tried not to dwell on his concerns as he found his way to the locker room and stowed his helmet. Taking a detour to the bathroom, he relieved himself and wet down his hair. He straightened his tie as well, because he took pride in his looks. He wanted to make a good showing for his new lieutenant if not his partner. Okay, and now he was just stalling. He forced himself out of the sanctuary of tile and quiet and headed to the bull pen.

Please, Jesus, don't let his new partner be a

douche.

Lieutenant Fuller seemed like a decent guy. As they waited for Diego's new partner to arrive, they sat in the lieutenant's office and chatted about Boston. His boss was obviously trying to put the new man at ease and give him pointers about getting around the area. So far, Diego had noted that he had to walk the Freedom Trail, but not to be discouraged if he crapped out somewhere around the Old North Church. Everybody did. Then there was the Aquarium, the Science Museum, and the Museum of Fine Arts, all of which sounded like places he'd go if he had kids or an appreciation for serious art. Neither of which he did. Fenway Park would be a great idea, if Diego wasn't a Yankee's fan. Sadly, from the lieutenant's point of view, he was.

The lieutenant was starting to branch out into Salem and Plimoth Plantation when Diego's partner finally showed up. To be fair, the guy wasn't late. Diego had a habit of always being early. He stood to greet Ronan Callaghan as they were introduced. As they shook hands, they sized each other up. Diego was taking Ronan's measure and could tell by the look in the other man's eye, he was doing the same. It rankled that the Boston man was a few inches taller, but while Puerto Rico had many things to recommend it, growing tall people was not one of them. On the other hand, Diego packed more muscle. Callaghan had that long, lean look to him, whereas Diego had played high school football.

"Have a seat, Callaghan," the lieutenant said. "I know having your partner go out so suddenly is disconcerting, but the timing is great in that Nieves here needs one."

Diego gave Ronan a sharp look. "What happened?" He hadn't heard of an officer going down.

Ronan gave him a wry grin. "Twins."

"Excuse me?"

"Vicki and her husband have been trying for a while to have a baby, and just their luck, it's twins. She's on bed rest."

"Oh. Well, please tell her congratulations from me, and I'll pray to Saint Margaret for her safe delivery."

Ronan narrowed his eyes. "I thought Gerard was the patron saint for pregnant women."

Diego shrugged. "Some say that, but my mother says that makes zero sense. Margaret was a woman and a virgin. She's a better saint for the job."

"A *virgin* is a better saint for the job?"

"Gerard was supposedly a virgin, too."

Ronan looked like he was ready for a Catholic throw down. A loud throat-clearing from the lieutenant cut him off.

"Gentlemen, if we are done with the religious instruction...? I'm sure we all wish Detective Sergeant Villas well in her pregnancy. In the meantime, you're going to be partnered. Do you have any active cases, Callaghan?"

"No, sir. We'd just wrapped one up when she started feeling bad."

"Fine, go help Nieves get settled in at Villas' desk for now and find something useful to do until you catch another case. Given the way this summer is going, that should be in about thirty seconds. Dismissed."

"Yes, sir," they said in unison.

"Oh, and Callaghan?" the lieutenant called out a

second later. "Nieves is primary as he's more senior even if he did get his experience in New York."

Ronan hesitated a second, casting a glance at Diego. His expression was unreadable. "Yes, sir," he finally said and walked out.

Diego let Ronan lead the way across the bull pen. He found himself looking at a messy desk. Ronan plopped down in the chair at the desk opposite his. It was equally messy. The guy picked up a large iced coffee and slurped on the bright orange straw sticking out of it.

Diego sat gingerly at his new desk and surveyed the paper and other detritus strewn over the surface. "I thought you said you'd cleared all of your cases."

Ronan looked at him over his straw. "We did. Vicki likes to hang onto stuff that doesn't have to go into the file. You know, background info, research, shit like that. Plus she's a squirrel and never throws anything away."

Eyeing what looked like stuff you'd find in Happy Meals, Diego understood exactly what his new partner was saying. "What am I supposed to do with all of this?"

Ronan shrugged. "Stuff it in a box. I'll take it to her house, and she can sort through it. It will give her something to do while lying around. She's already going crazy. Hates daytime television."

"I don't suppose as her former partner you'd like to…" He made a sweeping gesture at the desk and gave Ronan a hopeful look.

Ronan grinned back at him. "Not a chance. I have my own crap to deal with."

That was certainly true. "How do you stand

working with all that heaped up?"

Ronan only shrugged and went back to sipping his drink. There was no chance to push the issue. A uniform came up and handed Ronan a slip of paper. His partner's laid-back demeanor didn't change, but he stood up. "We've got a DB. I drive."

Diego stood up, too, his nerves jangling at the idea of going out into the field. He ruthlessly shut down the feelings. If he couldn't handle taking a case, then he was done being a cop. Besides, this was new territory. The whole point of moving to Boston was to take his therapist's advice to change up his environment, to change up his thought patterns. "Fine by me, Callaghan. I didn't think you'd want to ride bitch on my bike anyway."

As soon as he used the crude expression, he regretted it. His mother would have slapped him up the back of his head for being so disrespectful. He was letting his worry about his partner looking down on him put him in a defensive position. That was a stupid way to start their relationship and his new job. Not wanting to compound the problem, however, he didn't back track on his comment.

Ronan looked at him from the corner of his eye. "You have a bike? What kind?"

"Harley." He didn't add the "of course" although it was implied in his tone.

"Nice."

Okay, so points for him. He'd managed to impress his partner over his choice of ride. Juvenile to be sure. He'd take them anyway.

Ronan's car was a fairly nondescript, mid-sized standard issue coated in a fine layer of dust. The inside looked like the mobile version of Ronan's desk. Diego gingerly slid in and buckled his belt even as he kicked a fast food bag away. Ronan did the same and started the car, all while still sipping his coffee. Of course, the cup holders between them were jammed with change and crumpled napkins, but still.

"You want me to hold that for you?" While it was the last thing he wanted to do, it beat crashing.

"Naw, I'm good."

Ronan peeled out of the lot, working the steering wheel as if he was on a Sunday drive. The streets of Boston had earned their reputation, although as a New Yorker, Diego sneered inwardly at the idea it was the worst traffic in the country. Ronan hit the siren and maneuvered around the other vehicles with a skill Diego had to admire even putting aside the fact that it was done one-handed.

"Where are we going, exactly?" Diego asked, resisting the urge to cling to the dashboard.

"To the river, by the Hatch Shell."

New as he was to Boston, Diego understood that the river was the Charles and the Hatch Shell was the outdoor venue for concerts, most especially by the Boston Pops Orchestra on the Fourth. He decided not to ask any more questions and let his partner concentrate on not crashing.

The crime scene was easy to spot. A couple of marked cars and an ambulance were already parked on the side of Storrow Drive, a roadway too narrow and congested for parking. Traffic had started to back up even though it wasn't rush hour. A beleaguered uniform directed harried drivers away from the blockage. Diego got out on legs slightly shaky due to the ride over and those damn nerves of his. He took what he hoped was a subtly big breath and let it out slowly.

He could do this.

Ronan ambled up to the uniforms and the other responders, greeting most of them by name. The reaction from the others was telling. Big smiles and hand shaking told him that his partner was well-known and well-liked. He supposed that wasn't a bad thing. As Ronan stopped to question some of them about details, or maybe just to talk about sports scores, Diego continued on to the victim. Everyone moved away as he approached, giving him his first look at the DB. Male of so far an indeterminate age. A woman leaned over him on her knees. Diego saw blonde hair in a ponytail and a shapely ass.

He walked around the prone figure, taking in the visible details. Shoes barely holding together, grease stained pants that looked like they'd come out of a dumpster topped with a hole-filled T-shirt and grimy hands and arms. All that was immediately overshadowed as he caught sight of the gaping wound from ear to ear. The woman who was examining the corpse sat back on her heels and looked up at him. Diego's attention was immediately stolen by pale, flawless skin, high cheek bones, and vividly blue eyes.

The woman flashed him a smile. "Hi, I'm Cassidy Barnes, the new M.E."

The nascent smell of human decay wafted up to him. Despite that little horror, his body was on high alert, the lure of Dr. Barnes' gaze overwhelming anything else. It took a few seconds before Diego's mind and tongue started working enough for him to answer her.

"Um, hi," he said, squatting down on the other side of the corpse. Damn, he was usually smoother than that with women. "I'm Detective Sergeant Diego Nieves. I'm new, too," he added with a smile that usually resulted in at least a phone number. Not that he was trolling for a date over a dead body, but Holy Mother of God, this woman was too enticing to ignore.

"I'm thinking you're new to Boston and not just the force. Your accent is subtle, but I'd say New York?"

"Correct."

"Well, I'm Boston born and bred, just new to the coroner's office."

Her accent wasn't the thick stereotypical one he'd heard from some people in the area. She sounded more cultured, and he'd bet the diamond studs twinkling in her earlobes were genuine. She probably came from a section of Boston that was lined with trees and quiet. Classy and expensive, yet her expression was open and inviting.

Diego wrinkled his nose as he looked down at the body. "I hope this isn't your first." 'Cause that would suck. The man hadn't been in the water apparently as his body was dry and didn't look bloated. But that was a small mercy. It was an ugly corpse to view.

Cassidy sighed. "Not my first. Although I won't know for sure until I've had a chance to do a thorough autopsy, my initial guess is that this man died from having his throat cut."

The understatement and its dry delivery caught him off guard. It seemed incongruous with what he saw that she would be capable of cracking a joke while examining gruesome remains. He understood the impetus, of course. Gallows humor helped to keep the horror they dealt with every day at bay. He stifled a laugh as someone walked toward them and stopped at the head of the body. Glancing up, Diego saw Ronan. His partner had ditched his coffee, thank God, and was looking wide eyed not at the DB but at the ME.

"Hi," Ronan said, squatting down. "I'm Ronan Callaghan, Nieves' partner."

Cassidy gave him the same winning smile she'd given to Diego, so maybe she was just friendly with everyone and his shot at getting her to go out was a long one.

"Callaghan, huh? That's a name I've heard before."

"Oh?" Ronan's expression became guarded and his tone a little chilly. His body stiffened just a bit, as if he were bracing for a fight. That was odd.

"Yes, I met a Daire Callaghan on my first case."

Just like that Ronan's expression and body language changed again. "Oh, yeah, my older brother, emphasis on the *old*," he said with a charming smile that probably got him not just women's phone numbers but the women themselves.

Cassidy raised her eyebrows. "Really? He seemed younger than me."

Before Ronan had a chance to back pedal on his age comment, Diego jumped in. He was pretty sure he was older than Ronan, and while he might not be the doctor's age, he happened to like more mature women.

"Please excuse my partner, doctor. Given his young age, his frontal lobe just finished growing. He doesn't appreciate the appeal of maturity."

Cassidy grinned at the statement. Ronan's mouth opened for a retort. Figuring they'd wasted enough time, Diego overrode him. "So, the victim?"

Both Cassidy and Ronan shifted their attention to the body.

"Middle-aged male, or close to it, between forty and forty-five, I'd say," Cassidy began. "He's been dead for about ten hours, putting T.O.D. at around midnight. Looks like a single stroke of a sharp blade from left to right, so you're looking for a right-handed killer. I'll have to do a tox screen, but the lingering smell of alcohol indicates he may have been drunk when killed."

"I'm told he had no I.D. on him," Ronan jumped in, his tone all business and his look serious as he gazed at the corpse. "Appears he was a vagrant."

"That's certainly what his appearance indicates," Cassidy concurred.

Diego was about to weigh in on the observation when he focused on the victim's hands. He got down on his knees to take a closer look, and at the fingers in particular. He held out his own hand without looking up.

"Can I borrow some gloves?"

"Sure." Cassidy slapped surgical gloves in his open palm.

Sliding them on both hands, he picked up the victim's and held it up for scrutiny. With rigor already setting, it was hard to lift it too close, so Diego stayed bent down.

"What's up?" Ronan asked.

"Take a look at his fingernails." Diego moved to his left to give Ronan room to slide closer. "As dirty as he is, his nails aren't torn. They look recently groomed, you know like with a nail clipper."

Ronan dropped to his knees and hunched over the hand. He nodded. "You're right." Scooting back, he gestured to the head that was angled back given the gaping hinge across the neck. "Can you please pull back his lips?" he asked Cassidy.

She did so gingerly, and Ronan peered at the teeth revealed. Ronan looked at Diego and gestured with his own head. "Take a look at his teeth."

Diego braced a hand on the ground and leaned over. While they weren't the best set of choppers he'd ever seen, the victim appeared to have all of them and they'd been cleaned on a regular basis.

"If this guy was homeless, it was a recent event in his life," Diego observed.

Ronan nodded his head. "I agree. Interesting. How quickly can you do the autopsy on smiley here?" he asked Cassidy.

She looked back and forth between the two of them, a thoughtful expression on her face. "I'll put it at the top of my list."

Ronan shot her a megawatt smile that turned his boyish charm up to an eleven, the bastard. "Thanks. Let me give you my number so you can text me when you have the preliminary results."

As he watched the exchange of information, Diego reminded himself they were working a case, not a bar, and that his focus needed to be on the victim, not his sudden desire to pound his new partner's face into the ground.

Chapter Two

Ronan cranked the A.C. in the car as he loosened his tie. After spending a couple of hours going over the crime scene and interviewing the jogger who'd spotted the body, he was as hot, sticky, and sweaty as he'd been earlier after his jog. His new partner, on the other hand, still had his suit jacket on and looked fresh as a daisy. Ronan eyed him with distrust. He wasn't sure the guy was human, and it was just one more point against him. Being from New York and undoubtedly a Yankee's fan had been the first strike. Eyeing the new M.E. with obvious male interest was another.

Cassidy Barnes was an unexpected treat and a far cry from the other pathologists he'd worked with. He'd spotted her before he even reached the cadaver and had wrangled her deets from one of the other crime scene investigators before he introduced himself. Word was that she was not only new but had serious medical credentials and could practice anywhere she wanted. She was also really nice to everyone, patient with subordinates, and funny in an unexpected way. She was also, of course, gorgeous. He'd seen that fact for himself. And, drumroll please, not married, engaged, or even dating as far as anyone knew.

Maybe she was gay, but he didn't think so. He knew when a woman was into him, and the vibe from Dr. Barnes was a sexy "hi there" one. He was sure of it.

Unfortunately, he was equally as sure she felt the same way about his partner. The look in her eye when she stared up at Diego held the same gleam she'd aimed at Ronan, and that sucked. Either she was playing games or she liked them both. Neither possibility appealed to him. Plus, when he looked at Diego, it was like looking into a mirror. The guy held the same "I want to go there" expression as Ronan knew he did himself.

He pulled out into the heavy traffic of Storrow Drive with a hard yank of the wheel and grinned inwardly in satisfaction as his partner grabbed onto his "oh shit" handle. Ronan decided it was a good idea to put thoughts of Cassidy aside and concentrate on the case for a while. "So what do you think?"

"I think our victim either fell on hard times within the last forty-eight hours or so and turned into an instant homeless man or there's something more going on here."

Damn, although Ronan was inclined to find fault with the transplanted New Yorker and potential dating rival, he had to admit the man had excellent police skills. The observation about the fingernails had been dead, so to speak, on.

"Yeah, I agree. On the surface, he looked like every other dead vagrant I've ever seen, and I've seen quite a few. It's too easy for them to die of exposure or get hit by a train or to end up in a deadly fight over booze or even shoes. I hate how we do such a lousy job taking care of our own, especially the vets. This guy could have easily been one if you looked at only the clothes and the layer of dirt. You were right, though, about the grooming underneath the grime. And it wasn't just the nails and the teeth. Did you look at his hair?"

Diego nodded. "It was unkempt, but not matted and not very long. It had been trimmed recently."

"Yeah."

He cut over to exit off Storrow and head to the precinct. He was hoping to have a chance to change his shirt and clean up a little before the lovely Cassidy was ready to see them. He always kept spare clothing in his locker, and he wanted to look his best when he went to the morgue. He was hoping to have a chance to ask her out. That is, if his partner didn't get his shot in first.

Stealing a glance at his passenger, Ronan could see why a woman would be interested. Diego was handsome in an exotic way, with short dark hair, olive-toned skin, and brown eyes. Ronan's hair was equally dark, and he knew his blue eyes made for a nice contrast to that. But his skin tended to be too pale if he didn't spend some time in the sun. He had a few inches on Diego, although the other man was more muscular.

And, comparing himself to another man was more "Mean Girls" than macho, so he should knock it the fuck off.

"The question is," he said to get his thoughts back on track. "If the guy wasn't really homeless, who the hell would go to the trouble of trying to make him look as if he were? Or was this some kind of weird-ass version of slumming it for him and the game got a little too real when an actual homeless man killed him for his money?"

"Perhaps the poor guy was mentally ill or suffering from dementia and wandered away from home," Diego offered.

"That's an interesting angle." Ronan pulled into the

precinct lot. "Look, I need to change. Standing out in that heat has turned me into a melting Popsicle. Why don't you check on the missing person files while I head to the locker room? I'll be quick about it and come give you a hand. Something might pop there before we get word from Cassidy."

"Sure. That's a good idea."

It rankled, even though it shouldn't, that while his new partner was the senior man of the two of them, he didn't pull rank and nix the plan because Ronan had suggested it. The guy was obviously secure in his position and didn't feel the need to throw his weight around. That was a good thing, so why did it irk him?

He shook off the feeling as he headed into the locker room and made short work of cleaning up. By the time he returned to his desk, Diego was in deep concentration on his computer.

"Nothing's popped so far," Diego said without looking up from the screen. "If the vic went missing recently, it wasn't from Boston or the surrounding area."

Ronan plopped into his chair and booted up his own computer. "Maybe he hopped a train from somewhere else."

Diego looked over at him skeptically. "Does anyone actually do that anymore?"

"Sure," Ronan replied with a shrug. "It's harder these days, but it happens."

Diego rocked back in his chair. "Did you notice the shoes?"

"What about them?"

"He wasn't wearing any socks, so it was easy to see how they fit on his feet and they looked about a size too big to me."

"That doesn't necessarily mean anything. Homeless people make do with what they can."

"True, but it will be interesting to see if the vic's feet show problems from wearing the wrong size. That's something that should be in the M.E.'s report."

Coincidently with the mention of the lovely Cassidy, Ronan's phone pinged. Pulling it out, he read the text and grinned. "Post-mortem's about done. Cassidy says to come over any time, and she'll give us the run down."

"Cassidy?" Diego said with his eyebrows raised.

"Dr. Barnes, if you prefer." Ronan gave him a pointed look.

Diego returned it. "I prefer Cassidy, myself."

"Then we're of a mind, there."

They sat staring at each other for a few seconds, stupidly and with way more testosterone than should permeate any room in the twenty-first century, but there it was. Diego glanced away first as he stood up. Ronan in no way took that as a sign of the other man's weakness or capitulation. He stood, too, and followed his partner silently out to the car. By unspoken agreement, they didn't talk about anything on the way to the morgue. When they entered the chilly and creepy room where Cassidy had their vic laid out, she greeted them with a friendly smile and a wave for them to come join her by the corpse.

That smile hit Ronan low in the gut, putting a momentary hitch to his stride. Even all suited up in her protective autopsy gear, her figure was on full display. She wasn't very tall even for a woman, but she possessed the traditionally sexy hourglass curves. He liked the look, never having developed a taste for tall and thin. The way her breasts filled out the top of her scrubs made his palms itch. He reflexively curled his fingers, as if grabbing a handful. A small exhalation of air beside him confirmed Diego had a similar reaction. The fucker.

Ignoring his partner, Ronan poured on the charm, greeting Cassidy back with a wide smile. "Hey, Doc, what do you have for us?"

Turning back toward the body, Cassidy started her report. "I can definitely confirm he was killed by a single slash to his throat that cut through his trachea. Given the one-shot precision of the swipe, I'd say the killer knew what they were doing."

"They?" Diego asked as he and Ronan walked to the other side of the table.

"Sorry, I'm being gender neutral in my assumptions in a grammatically incorrect way. I have no reason to believe there was more than one person involved. There were no signs of a struggle, no bruising or abrasions."

"He knew his killer," Ronan surmised.

"Or they caught him by surprise," Diego amended.

Cassidy nodded. "One or the other. The contents of his stomach indicate he had a nice last meal, fish and vegetables. There appears to be alcohol in his system, but I won't know how much or whether he ingested any drugs until the tox screen results come back. You know that takes a while." She wrinkled her nose in an adorable fashion. "My gut's telling me he wasn't drinking for long, and his body shows no signs of alcoholism."

"You mean he was in good health?" Diego asked.

"Fairly, yes, given his age. There're no signs of cirrhosis or other liver disease. He has some plaque in his heart, but no more than a lot of guys his age. His muscle tone was good, although he could have stood to lose about twenty pounds."

"What was the condition of his feet?" Diego prodded some more.

Cassidy shrugged. "He could have used a pedicure, I suppose. Again, nothing out of the ordinary for a man his age."

"So, it didn't look as if he'd been wearing shoes that didn't fit for a long time?"

"No, and I did notice the shoes and his clothes in general didn't fit him well."

Leaning into the body more, Ronan peered at the guy's face. "I haven't seen too many homeless men that are well fed." He cocked his head to get a better look. "This guy looks familiar to me."

Diego moved closer to Ronan and scrutinized the guy, too. "You mean you busted him once or maybe just rousted him from someplace when you were in uniform?"

"Maybe." There was this weird niggling in the back of his head that said this man was important in some way. The memory of when, where, and how he might have seen him slipped away as soon as he tried to take hold of it. It was maddening.

Finally, Ronan gave up and straightened. "It's not coming to me. Hopefully, we'll get a hit on his fingerprints on the Fed's IAFIS." He flashed a smile at Cassidy. "Anything else you can tell us?"

Cassidy blinked back at Ronan stupidly for a second or two, the force of the guy's smile killing a few brain cells.

Well, yes. When you smile at me like that, my heartbeat speeds up and my knees go weak. Classic signs of arousal.

Despite the cool temperature of the autopsy room, her cheeks felt flushed and she was damp between the legs. This was so not good. She'd told herself her reaction to these men had been some bizarre aberration brought on by the gruesomeness of the corpse and the ungodly weather of the day. That excuse wasn't going to cut it now. She was well acquainted with Mr. John Doe at this point, and there was no heat and humidity inside to blame. It was libido, pure and simple.

Except nothing was simple about finding herself simultaneously attracted to two men. Perhaps her reaction was a rebound effect from dumping her fiancé of five years. She had studiously ignored the attractiveness of men who were not Thomas, being the good girl as always. She'd especially given overtly masculine men a wide berth, telling herself she preferred quiet intellectuals who went to the gym just enough to stay a healthy weight, but not so much to develop obvious muscle. Yeah, that had been a big fat lie. Men with strong physiques were her go-to fantasies these days.

These two cops were something right out of those fantasies, too. Ronan Callaghan was tall and sleekly muscled, the picture of boyish beauty with dark hair that was too long and curled around his ears and the nape of his neck. He looked like a guy who'd just rolled out of bed. His bright blue eyes actually twinkled when he turned his attention on her, which so far was non-stop since they'd met. The guy was full of Irish charm, and if there was a woman on the planet who could resist him, she'd be very surprised.

Diego Nieves had the dark and smoldering thing going on. A bit shorter and more thickly muscled than Ronan, he kept his hair on the short side, and everything on him was neat as a pin. He appeared to be the kind of guy who took great care of everything in his life, a serious guy, but one who promised an explosive time in bed. When he fixed his deep brown eyes on her, she knew she was the center of his attention.

Jesus, if she ended up going out with only one of them, she'd count herself lucky. The only fly in the ointment was, she was sure both of them were a few years younger than she was. As Diego had indicated at the crime scene, Ronan was maybe mid-twenties and Diego closer to thirty. Regardless, at thirty-two, she was older than both, not by a huge margin, just enough to be noticeable. Except neither of them seemed to care about that if the looks they gave her meant what she thought they meant.

"Dr. Barnes? Cassidy?" Ronan's voice permeated her sexual fog, and she remembered he'd asked her a question.

Crap, she needed to get her head back in the game. "Um, no, that's all I have of particular interest. No signs of recent sexual activity, either, if that matters. And there was what I'd take to be an old bullet wound on his side."

"How old?" This from Diego.

"Oh, hard to say, but it's many years old. Here." She lifted the sheet to show them.

The two men bowed down, heads almost touching, to look at the scar. That was another thing to recommend them both. Even though she could tell they were interested in her, they were still focused enough and dedicated enough to do their job thoroughly.

She felt stupid for her lapse in attention, although she was sure of her autopsy results. Details were her strength, and she loved solving puzzles. Healing people had its appeal, of course, and she'd done well as an intern and resident. When it came to a career path, however, being a medical examiner was the perfect fit for her. Too bad her parents didn't see it that way.

The cops straightened up. "Well, at least we know he didn't live a completely quiet life," Ronan observed.

"Yes, but that doesn't put us any closer to figuring out who he is," Diego replied. He smiled at Cassidy. "Thanks. I guess we've seen and heard enough. You'll let us know about the tox screen?"

Cassidy crossed her heart. "As soon as I hear."

He smiled again. "Thanks."

"Yeah, thanks," Ronan chimed in. "You're more fun to visit with than Morris."

She frowned at him. "Morris is a nice man."

"You're nicer. See you around."

"Good-bye," Diego added as he followed his partner out.

Pulling the cover more fully over the victim, Cassidy started to strip herself of the gear in the vain hope that shedding some of her clothing would make her more comfortable. Her reasoning was stupid because she knew the heat came from the inside. Although, hopefully with the men gone, her core temperature would return to normal.

Her hip started to vibrate. She poked through the surgical gown to grab her phone. She couldn't hold back a grin when she saw the caller I.D. "Hi, did you forget to ask me something?"

"As a matter of fact, I did." There was a hint of laughter in Ronan's voice. "I forgot to ask you if you'll go out with me."

Nerves fluttered in her stomach like angry butterflies. It had been years since a guy'd asked her out. She wanted to play it cool, but hard-to-get had never been her style. "I'd love to. When?"

"Tomorrow night? I thought dinner."

"Oh, not just drinks? Isn't that the way you kids do it these days. Make it for drinks and if we hit it off, we can always move onto dinner. If not, it's over fast."

Ronan chuckled. "First of all, what's with 'you kids'? You're not that old, Dr. Barnes. Second, I don't need the escape hatch of a drink date. I'm sure I want to have dinner with you."

The certainty of his tone shredded the butterflies in her stomach. "Okay, me too. What time?"

"Sevenish? It's hard to say for sure when I'll get free. How about I text you tomorrow afternoon to confirm the time and place?"

"Sounds good." She couldn't keep the smile off her face and was glad there was no one else around to see it. She was sure she looked goofy, way goofier than a woman her age should.

They said their good-byes, and as she pressed end, her face fell. Damn, she didn't have any more date clothes. Good thing the date wasn't until the next night. She had shopping to do.

****

"Son of a bitch! You just asked Cassidy out." Diego had caught the tail end of the phone call as he caught up to Ronan by the car. Asshole! He should have known the guy was pulling a fast one when he walked briskly ahead of Diego even with the sun still beating down on them.

Ronan shot him a smug look as he unlocked the door. "Yep. That a problem?"

"You know damn well it is. I saw her first." Shit, now he sounded like a teenager.

"Sorry, man, I didn't hear you call dibs."

"Seriously? That's so juvenile." He buckled his seat belt and was too pissed off to grab anything as Ronan executed his standard out of the gate start.

Ronan shrugged. "I'm not the one whining about laying claim to Cassidy. A concept, I might add, she'd find offensive."

"What are you, Gloria Steinem?" God, the more he spoke, the stupider he sounded. He should just shut up. And yet he didn't. "There's a bro code, or don't you guys up here in Boston believe in that sort of thing?"

"Depends on what part of the code you're talking about. Now, if you're talking about having your back in the field, then sure, you can count on me. But if it comes down to stepping aside so you can move in on a woman like Cassidy, forget it."

"So that's it? We're at war over this?"

"If you choose to see it that way." Ronan shot him another smug glance that rubbed Diego's last fucking nerve raw.

He took a deep and silent breath, using the relaxation techniques he'd learned in therapy to calm himself. He was too quick to anger since the worst night of his life, and part of coming to Boston was to break up old patterns. Fighting with his new partner over a woman, who was frankly out of each of their leagues, was a piss poor way to turn over a new leaf. Besides, there was no point in trying to get Ronan to step aside and for sure Diego wasn't going to do it. The better part of valor was to retreat and find a way to outflank him.

Satisfied with his plan of action, he forced his body to relax. "Naw, forget it. We have a murder to solve. This isn't high school."

Pulling up to a red light, Ronan shifted to look at him. "I've known you for less than a day, but somehow I find it hard to believe you give up that easily."

Diego gave him his most disarming smile. "If you choose to see it that way... Light's green."

Ronan hit the gas with a frown yet didn't bother to challenge Diego further. When they arrived back at the station, they had an email from the lead forensic tech giving them the good news that the vic's prints had matched someone in the Fed's database. Each of them had a copy of the message, and they sat at their respective desks staring at the mug shots and other information contained in the file.

"Seamus O'Malley? Ring any bells?" Diego asked.

The guy had been arrested pretty regularly starting at eighteen, and likely there were sealed juvenile records as well. The last arrest had been almost eight years ago when the man had been in his mid-thirties. It was obvious this was their vic.

Ronan didn't answer right away. He peered at his screen intently. "I know this guy. This last mug shot in particular is familiar, although the name doesn't mean anything to me." He shrugged. "Obviously, he's Irish, but it's not like all the Irish in Boston know each other."

Diego snorted. "Yeah, I get that. And there's no way you ever busted him. You weren't even a cop, I bet, the last time he was arrested."

Ronan went still. There was nothing overt about his reaction, yet the sudden tension in the man was palpable. "No," he replied with a slow shake of his head. "I was just out of high school."

Diego snorted again. "You're just a kid."

Ronan didn't react to the jibe. Instead he said, "The summer after I started college, my parents were murdered."

Oh, shit! Yeah, he'd caught wind of that fact already. "I'm, ah, sorry." He winced at how lame his apology sounded.

Sitting back in his chair, Ronan stared off in the distance. "I don't know why I just said that." He frowned and looked at Diego. "Sorry, that was a weird non sequitur."

"No, it wasn't. I poked at your age, and O'Malley's record took us back to around that time." He stopped talking because he wasn't sure what to say. For the first time all day, his cocky and charming partner looked vulnerable. Damn, it was easier to deal with him when he was acting like a bastard.

Ronan shook himself, and the easy smile returned. "Let's see if we can get an address on Seamus. I can't believe he turned over a new leaf and stayed out of trouble for nearly a decade."

Okay, if Ronan was going to act like nothing had happened, Diego would, too. "People do change, although in my experience rarely when they start that young and are so relentless about getting arrested."

They spent the rest of the afternoon digging into the possible residence of O'Malley, and while there were enough men in the Boston area with that name, none popped as their guy. Just after five, Ronan threw up his hands. "Maybe the guy was really homeless."

Diego frowned. "You don't believe that any more than I do. He's just managed to stay off the grid somehow while still living well enough to eat fish, brush his teeth, and cut his fingernails.

"Takes cash to do that without leaving a trail."

"Or living with relatives."

"Yeah, that could be it." Ronan stood up and stretched. "We should start hunting down relatives." He glanced at his watch. "I'm good for a few more hours. How about you?"

Diego hesitated. While he was willing to put in long hours to solve a case, he had a different plan for the evening. Fortunately, he was saved from making excuses. A uniform came up to speak with Ronan.

"Sergeant Callaghan requests the pleasure of your company, Ronan." The uniform grinned as he pivoted away.

Ronan groaned. "Sorry, we'll have to pick this up tomorrow. My brother has other plans for me it seems."

"Sure, no problem. See you tomorrow."

Diego made himself spend five minutes at his desk, neatening things up a bit before he left. He didn't have much time to put his plan into action, and it was a crap shoot as to whether it would work or not. But if it did?

He couldn't keep the grin off his face at the thought.

****

Cassidy came to a stuttering halt when she caught

sight of the man leaning against the motorcycle. He looked so different in jeans and a polo shirt snuggly hugging his torso. Both his arms and his legs were crossed until his gaze latched onto hers. He stood up straight and gave her a welcoming smile, although his aviator glasses hid his eyes.

She returned the look and walked over to him. "This is a surprise, Detective Nieves."

He tore the glasses off his face. "Diego."

"Diego." Stopping a couple of feet from him, she hefted her messenger bag higher on her shoulder and debated internally how to phrase the question on her mind. "Did you need something from my report?"

It was kind of a dumb question, but she really didn't want to assume he was there for her. Maybe he was waiting for some other woman.

"No." He dropped his gaze, as if embarrassed. "I was waiting for you. I'm hoping you're free for dinner."

"Oh. Um." Now *she* stared at the ground. The idea of a man hanging around her place of employment in the hopes of taking her out was kind of thrilling. No one had ever been so interested in her that he'd taken such a chance.

"How did you know I was still working?" she asked, looking up at him again.

He shrugged. "I'm a detective." This time when he smiled, there was heat in his eyes.

The look drove away thoughts of dinner and replaced them with thoughts of bed. God, what was wrong with her? She'd already accepted a dinner invitation with this man's partner. Going out with Diego seemed, well, unseemly. Didn't it? Perhaps

Diego didn't know about her plans with Ronan. It was only right she tell him, although a naughty part of her was disappointed at the idea of missing out on a date with each of them.

"Okay," she said. "I'll accept that cryptic answer. You do know, don't you, that I'm going out with Ronan tomorrow night?"

"Yeah, I know. I heard him call you."

"Doesn't that bother you?"

"If you mean would I prefer that you go out with me instead? Yeah, I must confess I'd like that. But, you know, we're all adults, and to be honest, Cassidy, you've been on my mind pretty much since I met you. Ronan and I knocked off work early enough that I thought I'd take a chance on seeing if you were free."

"As it happens, I am." She peered around him to peruse his bike. It was enormous, and there were two helmets sitting on the seat. "Were you thinking of taking me out on that?"

Shrugging again, Diego twisted around to grab one of the helmets. "It's a nice night. Why not?"

Cassidy frowned down at her cotton pants and sensible flats. "I'm not really dressed for it."

"Sure you are. I'll do all the work and go slowly. I got a recommendation for a restaurant a few blocks from here, so we won't be going far. What do you say?" The expression he flashed her was part sweet charm and part irresistible seduction.

Taking a deep breath, she said. "Sure, why not?"

"Great, here let me help you put this on." He stepped closer and lifted the helmet, then stopped. "This is going to get in the way."

Holding the helmet in one hand, he reached back

with the other to tug her scrunchy out of her hair. When his fingers lightly brushed her scalp, a small shiver ran up her spine. Her cheeks flushed as she took the elastic cloth from him.

The helmet was a serious one, not just one that barely satisfied the legal requirement. Once it was on her head, he lifted the visor and peered at her. There was no way in hell she looked anything other than dopey with it on, yet his eyes clearly telegraphed his interest. So did his jeans. There was a distinct bulge in front she didn't need a medical degree to understand.

Diego put his own helmet on, then swung one of his thickly muscled legs over the broad seat. He held out his hand to help her do the same. Being shorter, it wasn't as easy for her. Her bag made it a little more awkward as well. But once she was firmly in place, he started the engine. The bike was as loud as it was big, and the roar of it gave her a thrill.

Diego looked at her over his shoulder. "Hold onto my waist as tight as you can. Don't worry about squeezing me. I just don't want you falling off. And when I take a turn, lean into the turn with the bike, not against it. Got it?"

Cassidy nodded. She slipped her hands then her arms around his narrow waist, tentatively at first. Diego was, after all, virtually a stranger. She wasn't used to grabbing hold of men, even ones she knew really well, as she'd been raised to be reserved. Beneath his shirt lay hard abs. Her hands could count the six pack through the cloth. It was deliciously brazen to rub her palms across his hard expanse. When he let the bike leap forward, she hugged him more tightly, her uptight Boston upbringing be damned.

Her splayed legs curved around his small, tight ass, and her breasts pushed against his broad back. The tremor of the bike goosed her nerve-endings, in particular the ones between her legs. It was like riding the world's largest vibrator.

As promised, Diego navigated slowly down the streets. Given the sudden state of her arousal, she couldn't imagine what it would be like if he took her for a fast ride. Her pants clung to the leather seat by the wetness between her legs, which had nothing to do with the lingering heat of the day. Or even merely because of the bike's motion. It was the man she gripped making her so.

Her clit throbbed eagerly with every bump and grind. Her nipples had turned into sensitive points, enflaming her breasts with each rasp against Diego's shirt. With the visor still up, the wind whipped gently against her face. Instead of helping her cool down, it revved her up. The bike was an amazingly liberating and thrilling mode of transportation. Taking a ride with a hot man even more so.

The ride came to an end all too soon. Diego pulled over and parked the bike in a spot that wasn't really a spot, but there was no ticketing at night and, big as it was, the bike was still much smaller than a car. She had trouble getting off by herself, her legs a little wobbly and the seat being so wide. Somehow, he managed to help her off without her landing on her ass. When she took off the helmet, she shook her head, sending her loose hair flying around her face.

She laughed. "I always wanted to do that, like being in a hair product commercial. This is the first time I've had an occasion to."

Taking the helmet from her, Diego gave her a rueful look. "Really? With hair that silky, I would have thought you shook it all the time to drive men wild."

Cassidy rolled her eyes. "I have never driven men wild."

Diego reached out and tucked some hair behind her ear. He gazed down at her. "You're wrong about that."

Her breath caught, and she became mesmerized by his eyes. Once again, she saw within them how much he wanted her. It was disturbing to be the focus of such desire and almost sent her running away. Almost. Instead, to buy herself some time to pull herself together, she adjusted her bag and stepped onto the sidewalk. "So, dinner?"

Diego cleared his throat and joined her. He held both helmets in one hand, and they managed to cover the front of his pants. He got points for trying not to unsettle her too much, although she already knew he was aroused.

"Yes, dinner. I'm told the food here is authentically Italian." He passed her to open the door to the restaurant and usher her inside.

"Are you part Italian?"

He hesitated as he joined her, his expression suddenly guarded. "No, I'm one hundred percent Puerto Rican." The way he pronounced his heritage told her he spoke Spanish as well. He stared at her, as if waiting for a response.

She smiled back and gave a little nod of acknowledgment, not quite sure what he was looking for her to say. Or, maybe, she realized he was waiting for her to have a negative reaction. Could that be it? Like they were in West Side Story or something? God, had other women given him reason to worry about it? She was suddenly livid on his behalf and her own if that were true.

She held his gaze, willing him to see that his ethnicity was irrelevant to her. Finally, he smiled back. When the hostess approached, he asked for a table for two. Thank God, there was no wait because she was starving. Diego moved quickly to put the helmets down behind his chair so he could come and hold hers out for her. The gesture was so sweet and old fashioned. She beamed her thanks.

He sat opposite, the small square table separating them by a couple of feet. It was a homey place with cotton table cloths, low lighting, and a lit candle flickering in a squat glass container in the middle of the table. It was romantic in a low key way. She glanced at Diego over the top of her menu and allowed herself to appreciate how sexy he looked, with his dark hair and olive skin. His shirt exposed a hint of his chest, where a couple of curly hairs resided. She'd never touched a man who had chest hair. Her fingers tightened their grip on her menu as she imagined what it would be like.

Diego glanced up from his menu. "If you keep looking at me like that, Cassidy, I'm never going to be able to figure out what I want to eat. Other than you, of course," he added in a murmur before she had a chance to challenge his statement that she was looking at him in any particular way.

She gasped in shock, the titillated kind, not the actually outraged kind. No man had ever said anything that provocative outside of bed or inside it. Naturally, Thomas hadn't, being so proper he barely managed to indicate he wanted sex at all. There was no chance to respond further because the server stepped up.

They both ordered a glass of Chianti, and Cassidy went with her usual Italian choice. "I'll have the fusilli Bolognese, please." Her taste buds tended toward the unadventurous.

"*Linguini fra diablo*," Diego said.

"That's a bold choice. It sounds too spicy to me."

Diego folded his arms on the table top, leaning in closer. "I like hot things." His tongue did a slow swipe of his bottom lip while his eyes were focused like lasers on her. She didn't miss his deliberate use of the synonym.

"Oh?" Heat flashed through her, and she took a big gulp of her ice water. "Is, um, Puerto Rican cuisine *hot*?" Wow, she was really bad at flirting.

Diego didn't seem to notice or care. "When it wants to be." His voice was low and seductive. He knew exactly what he was doing.

Cassidy was saved from coming up with a suitable reply by the server bringing their wine. Raising his glass, Diego leaned in even closer. "To the beautiful woman who agreed to have dinner with me." He brought the glass to his lips, and she watched as his throat worked the liquid down.

Oh, God, she was completely out of her depth. Instead of trying to come up with an equally complimentary toast, she gulped down some of the wine. Long minutes passed as they drank their wine and waited for dinner to arrive. Diego did most of the talking, amiable chatting about nothing in particular. She appreciated his giving her some space instead of continuing his seduction. She must have looked as awkward as she felt. She tried to stare playfully at him, but it was no good. She wasn't going to be able to be blasé about this impromptu date.

"I think this would be a good time to confess something," she said when there was a lull in the conversation. Diego raised his eyebrows, but otherwise gave her the space to continue. "I haven't been on a date in over a year, and before that, I'd been engaged for five years." She left out the part about how her fiancé had also been her boyfriend since college. It was just too pathetic to provide those additional details.

Diego twirled his glass thoughtfully. "Really? Then I'm even more flattered and grateful that you agreed to break your fast, as it were, with me. Thank you."

Seriously? "I don't think you're getting my point." Her explanation was interrupted by their meals being served. Her dish smelled delicious, and hunger drove her mouth to do something more urgent that speaking. She moaned over her first bite. It was delicious.

"I think we're going to have to add certain noises to the list of things you can't do around me, Dr. Barnes. Unless..." He paused with a morsel of food on his fork. "It's your intention to drive me insane."

Cassidy rolled her eyes at the comment, even though she was secretly thrilled at his compliments. She eyed his fork as it zoomed in on her. "No, thanks. I'm not used to spicy. I'm more of a New England bland kind of eater."

"I call bullshit," he replied with a grin. "Just try it."

She knew a dare when she heard one, and she was stubborn and competitive in her own way. Leaning forward, she opened her mouth and slid the offering into it with a delicate scrape of her teeth. At first, all she tasted was complex and delightful flavors. Then a tingling hit the back of her tongue as she swallowed. It made her flush from head to toe and revived the low level arousal that lingered after the bike ride.

"What do you think?"

She lowered her eyelids and leaned toward him again. "More, please."

Chapter Three

Diego gladly forked up more of his dish and fed it to Cassidy. The expression on her face and the little moans of pleasure she made each time she chewed were like a vice tightening his cock. Sweet Jesus, she was driving him mad.

The impulse to try to waylay her for a date hadn't given him time to appreciate what he'd be getting into. He'd almost dumped his bike on the pavement when her hands slid around his waist. Just that small amount of touch on a typically low sensitive area of his body had been a shot to his dick. Then the feel of her curved around him, hugging his ass with her hard nipples brushing against his back, had frayed what was left of his control.

This was supposed to be a nice, getting-to-know-you kind of dinner, not an exercise in torture. All he could think about now was getting her into bed. That was so not his style. Very simply, he wasn't that easy. Sex on the first date wasn't something he typically did or even thought about. He liked to get to know a woman before becoming intimate. Maybe it was a product of being raised by strong women, but he thought it was disrespectful to try to jump a woman first thing.

His cock apparently had decided his old style was going to change along with his new job. It had only one thing on its tiny mind—fucking Cassidy. It was going to have to learn to live with disappointment, however. Even if he were willing to toss caution to the wind, the lady wouldn't. Hadn't she just told him she'd been out of circulation for a long time? Engaged for five years? What kind of a dope was that guy not to leap at a chance of putting a ring on her?

He squirmed in his chair. "Seems like you're not as bland as you think."

Cassidy sat back in her chair heavily. "Color me amazed. I thought I knew myself."

"I'm glad I could introduce you to something new."

"More than one thing—first bike ride, first spicy food." She shrugged and picked up her own fork. "Who knows what else?"

Was that a hint of how the night might end? He didn't dare scrutinize it. Instead, he got down to cleaning his plate. Cassidy refused more of his meal and quickly polished off hers. When the server asked if they wanted dessert, they both refused, as they did the coffee. They briefly tussled over the bill. He won, of course, and happily handed Cassidy onto his bike once more.

The trip to her place was hell. Because she took the T to work, he didn't have to return her to her office. She directed him to the section of Boston he'd learned was called the Back Bay. It might have started out as landfill, but it was a toney section of the city now. Cassidy had him pull up to a beautiful brownstone.

He gazed up the façade of the building as he took the helmet from her. "Are these condos?"

"Um, no, I own the building. It's my home."

He looked at her with surprise. "The whole thing?"

She blushed. "Yes. It was my grandmother's. She gave it to me when she moved to South Carolina."

That's when Diego realized Cassidy looked like a million bucks because she probably had a million bucks, or two. Or three. Jesus, she was way out of his league in many ways. None of that meant squat to his dick, of course. The damn thing just pictured five floors where they could fuck all night.

"Wow, it's beautiful." He was suddenly unsure of what he should say or do next. "Thanks again for having dinner with me." He made it sound like a good-bye because he didn't want her to think he expected anything more from the evening. If it ended here, it would be enough.

"Would you like to come in?" she asked almost before he'd even finished his sentence. "We could maybe have that coffee."

He looked hard into her eyes and saw the unspoken invitation in them. Shit, he had expected her to be the gatekeeper because he wasn't sure he had the willpower. If she was buckling, he had no chance to stand firm. "I'd like that, thanks."

He followed her up the stoop, into an exquisite foyer inlaid with marble flooring, and up a staircase of deep brown wood. As they reached the next landing, she stopped and turned. Her delicate hands pressed against his chest as she leaned into him. Her eyes sparkled, yet her cheeks pinked up, and she darted her tongue out to wet her lips.

"I have to confess I don't really want coffee." Her voice was low and breathless. "I'd rather continue up the stairs to my bedroom. If that's okay with you?"

Words lodged in his throat, and no amount of swallowing let them out. Instead, he wrapped his arms around her and pulled her in flush for a kiss. The moment his lips touched hers, she gave a small sigh and opened up for him. He needed no further invitation, slipping his tongue in for a long, lingering taste. He wanted to take a leisurely stroll through her mouth and was caught by surprise when the intensity ramped up in a millisecond.

Cassidy fisted his shirt as he squeezed her tight against him. His kiss turned feral, hot, eager, and almost desperate. A whimper from her echoed inside him, and his body recognized it for what it was—an invitation to take more, not a plea for less. He shifted his hands, skimming them down her back to yank her shirt from her slacks. Then it was all smooth, soft skin he stroked as he backed her toward the stairs. She wiggled her hands from his chest to clasp his waist, then mimicked his actions. Her hands were hot on the skin of his bare back.

The pads of her fingers sent a shudder up his spine. His cock strained in his jeans, and he couldn't help pressing it against her abdomen. Far from being shocked at his boldness, she purred into his mouth and rolled her hips to rub against him. He grunted and broke the kiss, his lungs needing to take a large breath. The woman clinging to him gulped in her own breath. She looked up at him with heavy-lidded eyes before diving in for another kiss.

They bumped into the bottom of the next set of stairs, yet neither of them was inclined to let go long enough to make it up to her bedroom. So they stumbled up while they groped and moaned. Diego turned them sideways to help get them up more easily and took the opportunity to cup one breast. His thumb flicked the hard point of her nipple. When she moaned, he worked the thumb under her bra to do it again. This time, she cried out. Jesus, he needed to get her to bed. Reluctantly, he let go of her breast to bend and scoop her up in his arms.

Cassidy squealed and dug her nails into his back as she clung even more tightly to him. The little prick of pain shot straight to his dick. He trotted them to the next landing, his armful of woman weighing little. He let go of her mouth only long enough to get directions.

"Here?" he asked, breathless from arousal, not the journey up the stairs.

"Uh-huh," she nodded, her lips brushing against the corner of his mouth.

Without a hitch in his stride, he carried her into her bedroom. Lights came on instantly, and he took a second to appreciate the convenience of motion-controlled systems. He registered frilly and feminine before hastening to the bed. He placed her on turned-down sheets and followed so that he never stopped touching her. For the next few minutes, he worked her shoes, his boots, and both of their shirts and pants off. All of this while ravaging Cassidy's mouth.

Once they were down to underwear, he concentrated on her breasts. God, how he loved breasts. Hers were covered in a simple flesh-colored bra that—yes, thank you, Jesus—had a clasp in the front. He flicked it open with thumb and forefinger and took one rosy nipple into his mouth. Cassidy rewarded him by arching up. She fisted what little of his short hair she could and pressed him harder against her chest. He nestled his leg between hers and humped his thigh against her clit. He sucked the hard nub in time to his rubbing and worked the other nipple with his thumb.

With a sharp cry, she convulsed against him. Her fingers clawed at his scalp and her legs flailed against him.

Holy shit, he'd made her come already. But that didn't slow her down. If anything, she moaned and writhed even more. "Diego, I need you inside me."

Need, not want. Her demand made his cock jerk. The head already peeked out from the front of his boxers. Reluctantly, he let her go in order to wiggle out of them. She twisted beneath him and, leaning over, pulled open the drawer to her nightstand. He saw the box of condoms and moved to take over the chore of grabbing one and sheathing himself. Thank God, she was prepared. He had one in his wallet, of course, but it was only one and he didn't think that would be enough.

As soon as he was ready, he slid her panties down her slender, creamy legs. The cotton was wet to the touch, and he sneaked a whiff before tossing them aside. She looked up at him with hungry eyes. Then she lifted her arms in invitation. He started to dive onto and into her, then made himself slow down and savor the moment. Urging her thighs farther open with his knee, he braced his arms on either side of her. He kept his gaze on her face as he slowly lowered himself and slipped his cock into her waiting pussy.

Wet as she was, he was met with no resistance. He thrust in balls deep. His reward was Cassidy once more arching up against him. When she wrapped her legs around his waist and clutched at his shoulders, he got the message. He thrust fast, hard, and deep, stoking them both. His orgasm built quickly, and he worked at holding it at bay. No way would he come before making her do so for a second time. He lowered his mouth once more to one of her hard nipples, laving it with lazy circles and quick flicks of his tongue before sucking on it.

That did it. She came in silence this time, her mouth opening into a wide O, as if the force of the orgasm robbed her of voice. Seeing what he did to her sent him over the edge, too, cum spurting out of him as her cunt milked him dry. He kept thrusting even when he was empty, the pleasure of being sheathed inside her too tempting to give up.

Finally, he found the strength and pulled out. He knew he should get up and deal with the condom, yet couldn't let her go. So he lay on his back and pulled her over to lie against him.

She came willingly and sighed contentedly as she slung an arm over his chest.

"I've never done this before," she confessed after they spent a minute regaining their breath.

It took a second for his foggy brain to register what she'd said. He lifted his head a bit to look at her. Her gaze was lowered. "What?"

"Had sex on the first date."

"Oh." He smiled with relief, although if she had been a virgin, he knew he'd at least satisfied her. "Me, neither," he confessed right back.

Pulling back a fraction, she stared up at him. "Really? I thought guys liked having sex on the first date. And on every one."

He snorted. "I guess that's true for a lot of guys, but it's never been my style. Until tonight."

She swirled his chest hair around her finger. "I guess I was a little pent-up. And...never mind."

"What?" When she shook her head, he nudged her. "Come on. You can tell me anything."

She propped herself up on her elbow. "It's just that I've always been really proper, you know? It's how I was raised, and Thomas, my ex, was a very reserved guy. Not someone prone to impulsive behavior."

Diego could believe that. What a moron. Underneath Cassidy's calm demeanor, was a hot woman. How could anyone miss that after spending time with her?

"Anyway, I was all set to marry him, the perfect guy for me as far as my family was concerned. And I was going to join my father's medical practice. Then one day...I don't know." She shook her head. "I woke up thinking is this it? Is this what my life is destined to be?"

She plopped back down, nestling her head on his shoulder. The small gesture of affection and easiness with him made him smile.

"I didn't want to be a GP. I wanted to be a medical examiner. I didn't want a nice, reliable guy who would hope, but never assume, sex on Saturday and maybe a blowjob on his birthday every year."

Diego barked out a laugh. "Wow, he sounds like a really nice and boring guy."

"I know, right? Anyway, I broke the engagement, although I don't think I broke his heart. I did break my parents' careful planning for me."

"Hey, it's your life, your decision." He knew that from experience. No matter what people had advised him, he knew he needed to leave New York and start fresh. But now wasn't the time to delve into the ugliness of his past.

Cassidy sighed. "Yeah, that's what I thought. I don't have regrets, either. I love my work. Doing autopsies is like helping to solve a puzzle. I feel like I'm doing something important."

"You are."

They were quiet for a few minutes, and just when Diego felt he should make a move to go, Cassidy's hand slid down to where his still sheathed cock messily lay against his thigh. She tapped at the root with her forefinger. "Think this guy is done for the night?"

Diego arched his brows. "No way."

She beamed up at him. "Awesome!"

****

Ronan bolted upright in bed. The remnants of his dream tried to slip away, but he grabbed hold and held fast. His parents. No, his father. He'd been dreaming of the man not right before his death. Sometime prior to that. Ronan had been a little younger, and he'd been coming out of Fenway Park after having the rare treat of being out with his old man alone, no older brother or younger one horning in on the attention. Being the middle child had been tough. The Sox had won, and his father had let him eat and drink himself sick. Ronan waved a big foam finger in perfect happiness even though at fifteen, he was really too old for such things.

Then his father had stopped suddenly, his demeanor changing from glee to something else. Stress, maybe, or even anger. Another man approached him, one that had the look of a guy who'd grown up mean and lived hard. His father had told Ronan to wait for him and dragged the other man off to the side, a steady stream of indecipherable words coming out. When the two men parted, his father had not looked happy. Ronan had asked who the man was and his father said it was nobody important, just someone who sometimes gave him helpful information.

It had been Seamus O'Malley.

The DB had been one of his father's snitches in the Irish mob. That one chance meeting had stuck in the recesses of Ronan's mind. Running a hand through his hair, he pondered the implications.

He knew why the information had come to him that night in his dreams. Daire had called him to the family home the previous night to work on their parents' murders along with Finn. They sifted through the files and boxes of evidence every once in a while, hoping to learn something new. Despite the fact that the effort hadn't yielded anything useful at the time, it had nudged his memory enough to dredge up what may or may not have been useful information for his current case.

He glanced at the clock. Five a.m. Knowing he wouldn't get back to sleep, or even if he did, it would probably be about five minutes before his alarm was set to go off, he decided to get up and go for a run. At least the weather should be cool. And no matter how the day went, he had his date with Cassidy to look forward to. That thought put a smile on his face.

The cheerful expression was still there when he rolled into the station. His new partner was already at his desk, although he didn't look like he'd had a very good night. With his chin in his palm, he stared stupidly at this computer screen and sipped at a large cup of coffee.

Ronan plopped down on his chair. He gave the man a toothy grin. "Morning, Nieves."

Diego sat up straighter and blinked at Ronan for a few seconds. "Oh, yeah, good morning."

Okay, so the guy sounded weird, and while he barely knew him, he thought something must be wrong. Given the day they had ahead of them, he decided it would be best to tackle the situation head on.

"What's wrong?" He took a long pull of his iced coffee as he waited for a reply.

Diego fidgeted as he glanced around. "I, ah, think I need to tell you something. Yesterday, it seemed like no big deal, just some friendly rivalry, or maybe unfriendly. I don't know," he added with a shake of his head. His gaze darted anywhere but at Ronan.

"What the fuck are you talking about?"

"The thing is, it is a big deal. She's a big deal."

A knot formed in Ronan's stomach. "She who? Cassidy? Spit it out, Nieves."

"I took her out last night."

"What!" Every head in the bullpen whipped their way. Ronan plastered a fake smile on his face and wheeled his chair closer to his partner. "What?" he repeated in a lower voice.

"I wanted to get the jump on you and took the chance she was free for dinner." Huffing out a breath, Diego leaned closer. "It turned into more," he added in almost a whisper.

Ronan stared back at him for a beat or two of his heart, reining in his fury. "You God damned son-of-a-bitch." He practically just mouthed the words.

"I didn't expect it to go that far because that's not my style." Ronan gave him a skeptical look. "It's not.

And it's not hers, but," he shrugged, "we just clicked. Anyway, I thought you should know. It was a dick move on my part, and it's also not usually my style to sneak around. We're partners, and we need to be able to trust each other. So…" He shrugged again.

Ronan didn't say anything. His brain had trouble working out his partner's confession and what it meant. Fuck, he liked Cassidy. Yeah, he'd rubbed it into the new guy's face because he couldn't help yanking people's chains sometimes, and the guy seemed too uptight and righteous even though they'd only known each other for less than a day. It hurt more than it should, given that he'd known Cassidy for even less time, but he'd been looking forward to seeing her again. Now he supposed that was off the table, although really, why should it be? Just because Diego was looking like he'd just fallen into a really bad romcom didn't mean Cassidy felt the same way.

He pulled his phone out of his pocket and sent her a text. *Are we still on for tonight?* May as well find out now where he stood.

Diego frowned. "What are you doing?"

"None of your fucking business," Ronan replied with the nastiest grin he could manage.

"You're not berating her over last night, are you?" Diego's tone took on an edge even nastier than Ronan's expression. Okay, so the guy got points for being worried about her.

"No, of course not. I don't hold women to some antiquated standard in which they can only date one guy at a time. Besides, I recognize that you're the asshole in all of this."

"Is that so?"

Before Ronan could answer, he got a text back.
Yes, looking forward to it.

This time the grin on Ronan's face was genuine. He texted "great" back to her and put his phone away. "I have some info on our DB."

Instantly, Diego lost his angry expression and went into professional mode. He got props for that, too. "What is it?"

"Believe it or not, I dreamt about him." As his partner's eyebrows went up, Ronan quickly explained about the guy being one of Ronan's father's snitches.

When he was done, Diego sat back and was silent for a while. "I have to confess I kind of heard about your parents being murdered before you told me."

Ronan sucked on his coffee, pushing the lump down his throat. The pain of this topic never went away. "Yeah, figured you might have. You probably heard, too, that some think my father was on the take." As he said it, he studied his partner's reaction.

Diego surprised him by holding up his hands and shrugging. "No, I hadn't, but cops are the worst gossips. I don't put much stock in rumors. And I've been the subject of the police rumor mill myself, so I understand."

"Sounds like a story you should tell me sometime."

"Sometime," he agreed noncommittally. "Anyway, where does this information lead us?"

"I don't know. The guy I remember was kind of scuzzy, you know? I can't quite square him with the well-fed and illness free stiff in the morgue. And why the hell wouldn't the guy have any arrests for such a long stretch, a stretch I might add, that pretty much coincides with my parents' murder?"

"All good questions. We need to figure out where he's been holed up all of these years. Let's start searching for relatives."

It was a solid plan, and putting aside their rivalry over Cassidy, they both delved into the files on O'Malley. They found the name of a sister, Colleen O'Malley Sullivan, and pulled up a current address on her fairly easily. They decided not to call first in case the woman was in on something less than savory with her brother and tried to avoid them. They hopped into Ronan's car and headed over to her home. Ronan parked a half a block away in front of a row of tidy houses in an old South Boston neighborhood.

"Let's hope she's home," Ronan said as they strode up the sidewalk.

"I don't know. With a neighborhood like this, it's usually a two-income family."

Diego was right, as no one answered the doorbell, although they could hear a yappy dog inside losing its mind over visitors at the door. A noisy neighbor poked her head out and got a wicked gleam in her eye when Ronan flashed a badge and asked if she knew where Ms. Sullivan might be. That led them to a bar around the corner.

"Jesus, we're not open for business this early in the morning," an older man shouted as they walked in.

Ronan once more flashed his badge. "We're looking for Colleen Sullivan."

Without shifting his gaze from Ronan and Diego, the man shouted for the woman. She came out, wiping her hands on a dish cloth. Rail thin in a way that spoke more of a cigarettes and coffee habit than a vegan diet and yoga, with hair bleached so many times it looked like straw, Seamus' sister was more like the man he'd remembered in his dreams. The O'Malley siblings had been raised in poverty.

Colleen stopped short when she got sight of them. Her eyes narrowed in suspicion.

"Colleen O'Malley Sullivan?" Ronan asked, once more holding up his badge.

She sighed. "Yeah, that's me—Colleen *Irish Irish*. What's up?" As she asked the question, her tone implied she already knew they came with bad news. He supposed with a brother like Seamus, who was probably a chip off the old block as these things usually went, her trouble radar was likely excellent.

"Is there a place where we can talk, ma'am?" Diego asked in the tone cops always used when delivering death notices to the next of kin.

She sighed again, more heavily this time, and looked down at her hands. "We can talk here, and I can guess what you have to say." She looked up at them. "Seamus is dead, isn't he?"

"Yes, ma'am," Ronan confirmed. "How did you know?" As he asked the question, he gently herded the woman to sit at a nearby table.

She didn't put up a fight. "I suppose I've been waiting for this news for a long time. Seamus was always getting into trouble, and even with the way he was the last time I spoke with him, I still expected it."

Diego took a seat next to her. "What do you mean about the last time? We know your brother had cleaned up his act. No arrests for the past eight years or more."

Colleen snorted. "Cleaned up his act? Seamus never changed."

"He got smarter, at least," Ronan injected.

"Not even that," Colleen replied with a roll of her eyes. "He just had less of a reason to get into trouble, that's all." When they both sat and stared at her, she explained. "A while back, eight or nine years maybe, he scored big, big enough for him to live off the grid. Paid cash for everything. He came around my place, showing off to me with rolls of dough, offering to buy me stuff. I told him to get lost. I didn't like the smell of that money. He'd done something really bad to get it, had to have. I didn't want nothing to do with it. You don't get that much by doing something good, at least not where we come from."

Now that was interesting news. What could a small time criminal like O'Malley have done to acquire so much money? When he asked that question, Colleen didn't have an answer.

"I don't know, and I didn't want to know. Even as he's trying to impress me with how generous he was being, he said we had to be quiet about it all. Said he wasn't supposed to be in Boston still but didn't feel like leaving. This was his home, and no one was going to push him out." She shook her head. "Idiot, trying to act like Mr. Big while he's peeking out my window blinds like he's afraid he was followed, sweat leaking through his shirt. I told him to get lost and stay that way. I didn't need the trouble."

"Was that the last you saw of him?" Ronan asked.

She stared off in the distance. "Yeah, that was the last time I saw him, but a few years ago, he sent me a letter. No return address on the envelope. I almost threw it away thinking it was junk mail 'til I realized it was his handwriting. He gave me his new address, but said I shouldn't try to contact him or give it out to anybody, even the cops if they came asking. He just wanted me to know where his stuff was in case something happened to him.

"He told me to memorize the address then burn the letter." With a snort she added, "Like that didn't make me nervous. Anyway, I did like he asked because I'm an idiot, too, I guess. He's my brother. Was my brother. I guess you can't get away from family that easily, no matter what."

"Did anyone, including cops, ever come around asking about him after that?" Diego asked a split second before Ronan had a chance to.

Colleen's gaze shifted around.

"It's important that we know," Ronan stressed in a gentle voice. She seemed spooked all of a sudden.

The woman blew out a breath. "Yeah, a couple of detectives did a few months after I got the letter, then again last year, although it wasn't the same two as before. They, ah, kind of leaned on me."

"Did they hurt you?" Diego asked in an even more gentle tone.

Collen rolled her eyes. "Nah, they just acted tough, tried to spook me about being charged with obstructing justice and other bullshit that don't cut any ice in Southie. Seamus and me were raised to keep our mouths shut. The only reason I'm telling you is 'cause he's already dead."

The woman's eyes misted up a bit, and she swiped impatiently at the tears forming. Even the biggest of rats usually left someone behind who mourned their passing at least a little. He could certainly empathize with her.

"I'm sorry, ma'am. Do you remember the

address?" She did and Ronan took down the information, thanked her, and left with Diego in tow.

"This doesn't feel right," Diego said, getting into the car. "From what I saw of his arrest record, the guy was neither bright, nor ambitious. A guy like that doesn't score big. And if he had money, he wouldn't be dressed like a homeless man."

"Maybe he blew through the cash and was living recently on the streets."

"His clothes would have been nicer if that were the case. It's not adding up."

"No," Ronan agreed. "It's not."

The address the sister had given them was in West Roxbury, a south west part of Boston that had a more suburban feel to it. It was a far cry from the Boston neighborhood the O'Malleys grew up in, a definite step-up for a guy like Seamus. They arrived at a duplex that was modest and tired looking, as if no one cared enough to keep it up. As luck would have it, the landlord was home. The man gave their badges the once-over and wasn't happy to hear they wanted to see where his tenant lived. He chomped on the disgusting remnants of a cigar while he let them in.

"Seamus O'Malley, huh? Told me his name was Steven Cabot, but I knew that was a crock. I know a mick when I see one." Looking at Diego, he added, "I can say that 'cause I'm Irish myself."

Ronan hid his irritation. They had bigger fish to fry, but Jesus, when would people get past these stupid slurs even of their own people? When Diego, who probably had been forced to develop a thick skin to epithets, gave the landlord a noncommittal look back, the man continued as he fished out his keys.

"I can't say I'm surprised he's dead," he said, still not taking the stogy out of his mouth. "He looked like every punk I grew up with in Southie. They all ended up at Walpole or the cemetery before hitting thirty." He pushed the door open and ushered them in.

"The state's maximum security prison," Ronan translated for Diego's benefit.

The place hadn't been cleaned in many months, but that appeared to be by design because there were pizza boxes and beer bottles lying around the living room, as if recently left there.

"The guy was a pig as you can see. But he paid his rent on time and in cash." The man grinned around the cigar. "Of course I declared every cent to the IRS."

"Of course." Ronan stepped farther into the home and looked around. Diego headed back to the kitchen. "Did he have any visitors that you know of, a girlfriend maybe?"

"He wasn't what you'd call a social kind of guy. I didn't see anyone hanging around, and he didn't date that I could tell. Unless you count working girls, that is. He had one or two of them over a month."

"I see. Well, thank you, Mr. Ahearn, we'll let ourselves out, and we'll have some uniforms come and cordon this apartment off until we're sure we've collected any evidence."

"Fuck, knew you'd say that. I watch all the *Law and Order* shows. I know how this works. I'll be lucky to rent it again by this fall."

The landlord left with a shake of his head.

As Diego was already in the back of the apartment, Ronan tackled the living room. There wasn't much to see, no personal mementos unless one counted the porn collection of DVDs. He rifled through the pile sitting on a built-in bookshelf, feeling dirty by merely touching the boxes. O'Malley's taste had been extreme, although none of them appeared to involve underage actors. That was something. Most if not all of them weren't properly closed which struck him as odd. If O'Malley was that sloppy, why bother to put the discs back in the case at all?

The thought occurred to him that the place may have been tossed. Messy as it was, it would be hard to tell. He stared around the room to see if there was any sign of greater chaos amid the mess.

"Callaghan, in here," Diego shouted.

Ronan hustled to the source of the voice and found his partner on his hands and knees on the threshold to a small closet. Clothing, dirty laundry he'd bet, was scattered around his partner. Diego got more props for rooting around in another man's soiled stuff. He was peering inside the closet with a small flashlight leading the way.

Ronan squatted beside him. "What am I looking at?"

Diego glanced up at him. "A hiding place."

Stretching his neck, Ronan saw the hole in the flooring. Diego had pulled up a few shortened planks of the old wood floor. A small square hole had been carved into the subflooring. Something hard and black lay inside. "Is that a laptop?"

Reaching into the hole, Diego pulled the object out. "Netbook."

"Same difference. Interesting how O'Malley hid it."

"Very," his partner agreed.

"There's more." Ronan wedge himself between the other man and the door jamb to stick his hand in the hole. Under the computer was a stack of one hundred dollar bills held together by a paper bank band. Holding it up to his forefinger to measure its thickness, Ronan said, "About ten grand, give or take."

Diego whistled. "Nice chunk of change."

"Yeah, but not enough to live on for long. I wonder if he has any more hidey holes." Ronan scanned the room. It was as messy as the living room. "How'd you manage to find this one, anyway?"

"I've learned that people with a modicum of imagination hide things where they think others would be disgusted to look. I worked robbery for a while, and this woman stole a packet of diamonds and hid them in her box of tampons like I'd be too squicked out to look there." He shook his head. "I thought it was weird how O'Malley's dirty laundry was jammed in the closet. Seems like he'd just leave them on the floor where he took them off, given the state of the rest of the apartment. The place where the floorboard had been cut was easy to spot once I cleared the clothing away."

Ronan stared at the size of the hole again. "Looks like he might have hid a lot of money at one time. Even given the space taken by the laptop, sorry, *netbook*, if he had hundred dollar bills, he could have easily fit tens of thousands in here."

Diego shook his head. "I still don't understand what he could have done or been in on that would have yielded that much of a pay-out. And with that much left hiding here, there's no way he was out on the streets. Even if he'd run out completely, he would have hung around here until the landlord got him evicted. I bet that takes months here the same way it does in New York."

When Ronan nodded, Diego continued. "Dirty and smelly as they are, these are decent clothes. He'd have been better dressed than he was when we found him."

Ronan rubbed at his chin. "I got the feeling out in the living room that this place has been tossed. I know it sounds crazy, but I swear someone opened up all of his porn DVDs."

Diego gave him a thoughtful look. "Sounds like they were looking for something in an effort to tie up a loose end, covering their tracks."

"God, the infamous 'they.' Who are they?"

Diego stood up and Ronan followed suit. "You said O'Malley was one of your father's snitches? Is there anyone we could talk to that would have known him back then, O'Malley that is? Maybe your older brother?"

Ronan smiled at the thought. "Naw, Daire was a shiny new cop when our parents were killed. He wouldn't have known anything about my father's informants. Uncle Jack was already in a wheelchair by then, and he was a beat cop anyway. Never had a reason to deal with snitches." He wracked his brain for anyone else, then smacked himself when the obvious came to him. "Of course, I'm an idiot. Uncle Connor."

"Jesus, how many of you are there?"

Ronan treated Diego to a nasty grin. "Do you mean Irish or just Callaghans?"

Diego winced. "Never mind. Forget I asked. Who is Uncle Connor?"

"He was my father's partner, so not really an uncle. Just a really good friend, except like a lot of my father's really good friends, he made himself pretty scarce once the rumors started flying. None of them wanted to be tainted as bad cops."

Because it infuriated him as it always did when he remembered how his father's name, and his mother's by association, had been dragged through the mud with whispered innuendos, he paced away with clenched fists. He hated showing his darker emotions to others, preferring people to see only the carefree part of him.

His new partner had other ideas. Instead of giving him space, he trailed after him. "Didn't anyone stand up for him?"

"Uncle James. That would be Mr. Police Commissioner, sir, these days. He's been around my brothers' lives and mine all these years since the murders, although he's discreet about it, if you ask me."

"Jesus," Diego gasped at Ronan's name dropping. "You really are some kind of Boston police royalty."

"Yeah," Ronan agreed ruefully. "Except it's like being from the part of the family descended from the executed traitor. Sometimes, I think the only people who still believe my father was a good cop are my brothers and our cousin, Regan, and her father, Jack." With a shake of his head. "I guess you can add Finn's boyfriend, Michael Caruso."

Diego stepped in front of him. "You can add me to that list, too."

Ronan was incredulous. "Seriously? You've known me for like a day. Why would you believe a fucking thing I say or even care?"

"I told you, I know what it's like to have cops whispering about you when your back is turned and get the facts wrong because the truth is either too awful to face or not awful enough to interest them."

That was the second time his partner had alluded to some trouble he'd had in what Ronan could only assume was his time as a New York cop. There was a story there, and damned if he didn't want to hear what it was. But now was not the time. "Okay, I get that. And, thanks. Anyway, I'll ask my Uncle Jack, who really is my uncle, if he can set up a meet with Connor. He's still on the force, I think, although working some desk job."

"Good." Diego nodded. "In the meantime, let's take this place apart. Who knows, maybe there's another hiding place."

Ronan grimaced. This wasn't going to be fun. But he had his date with Cassidy later to look forward to, that is, if his partner didn't somehow manage to beat him to the punch again.

Chapter Four

Slut. No, that wasn't true. She wasn't being fair to herself.

Cassidy stared back at her face in the restroom mirror at work. Her mother would think so, of course. Her mother, however, had also thought it was fine for Cassidy to have the longest engagement in the history of humanity. She had readily backed Thomas when he'd said he wanted to wait until they were done with their residencies in separate cities. Once they were back in Boston establishing their practices, they could throw the lavish affair that both families wanted, followed by a two week honeymoon in Europe. Then they'd come back and set up house in Weston or Wellesley or maybe Lincoln, one of the nice western suburbs so that they had the perfect home to bring their 2.5 children into when the time was right. So sensible and so utterly boring and unsatisfying.

No one seemed to think it important that the two of them spend time together, share intimate moments to strengthen their relationship. No one that is except Cassidy. At most, she'd seen her fiancé once a month depending on their hectic schedules, and the need for down time to get extra sleep always trumped their seeing each other. She had spent close to four years with mostly her vibrator for company, and as dedicated and diligent as her rabbit had been, it wasn't the same

67

as a flesh and blood man playing her body. It had finally occurred to her that, not only was self-gratification an unsatisfying way to spend early adulthood, it was also *more* satisfying than being with Thomas. The revelation had been her wake-up call.

Being with Diego last night had been the confirmation she'd made the right decision. God, her body still hummed with the excitement he'd stirred. She'd come so fast and hard with him and had been up and ready to go so quickly, that she understood she'd never really experienced sex the way she should have. The night had been eye-opening and knee-weakening. She'd all but floated through her day with the lingering effect of what, six orgasms, seven? She'd lost count. They'd made love three times before Diego limped out and she'd come at least twice each time. Wow, talking about making up for lost time.

Tonight she had a date with bachelor number two, and Ronan pushed her underused sexual buttons every much as his partner did. It was hard to believe she was going from practically a wallflower to a woman of infamy in twenty-four hours.

She was making some last minute adjustments to her make-up. Unlike her date with Diego, this one was planned, and she wanted to look her best. The only problem was that she felt a bit uncomfortable going out with someone else so quickly no matter how much she reminded herself that playing the field was perfectly legitimate. It wasn't as if she'd pledged undying love or even exclusivity to Diego.

The tricky part was that he and Ronan were partners. She didn't want to drive a wedge between them, however inadvertently. She had already decided she needed to come clean with Ronan before they started their date, in case he had a problem with it. Hiding it did no one any good. If he had a problem with it and wanted to cancel their date, she'd accept his decision with good grace.

With a last minute fuss with her hair, she left the women's room and grabbed her stuff. Ronan had said he'd meet her in the lobby. She stepped into the elevator and ignored those angry butterflies threatening to take wing again. Slow even breaths calmed her down enough that she was able to put a relaxed smile on her lips as she stepped into the lobby.

She stopped for a half a second and caught her breath when she spotted him. He had the Irish rogue look down pat with his dark wavy hair and easy grin. He'd dressed up a bit for her, wearing khaki slacks and a button down shirt. He'd been checking his phone, but now he focused all of his attention on her as she approached. The expression on his face said he was not only glad to see her, but he really saw her and not some random woman. The intensity of his gaze unnerved her and reminded her of how Diego had looked at her the same way. Which led to her remembering she was about to say something that would wipe the smile from his face.

"Hi," she said when they were only a few feet away.

"Hi, you look beautiful." His grin morphed into a heated smile.

"Oh, thank you." She flushed with the compliment. She'd dressed for the occasion, putting on a less than practical sleeveless sundress for the day with a drop waist and a hem cut on the bias for easy walking. She'd worn sneakers during work but now had on strappy gold sandals with a short spiky heel. Date clothes. She hoped he didn't ride a bike, too.

"Shall we go?" He held out his hand, as if to usher her to his side. When she hesitated, his smile dimmed. "Is something wrong?"

Cassidy wet her lips and noticed how Ronan's gaze followed the movement. "I need to tell you something before we leave. It might change your mind about tonight."

"I doubt it, but please go ahead."

"I went out with Diego last night. It was a spur of the moment thing, and…"

"I know. He told me this morning."

"He did? What exactly did he tell you?"

"That he'd dropped by on the chance that you were free and asked you out to dinner."

"Oh. Um, okay. Was that it?" Jesus, what was she asking him? Did she really want to know if Diego bragged about having sex with her? Besides, while she didn't know him well, she couldn't believe Diego was a fuck and tell kind of guy.

"That was it." Ronan frowned slightly. "He didn't give me details, and I didn't ask for any. It's none of my business what you two did last night."

Well, that was awfully mature of him. It flew in the face of everything she thought she knew about men. "Then it doesn't bother you?"

"The only thing that would bother me is if you're only going out with me tonight because you're too polite to cancel."

"Oh! No," she was quick to assure him. "I want to go out with you." She felt her cheeks heat up and had to fight to keep from cupping them with her hands. She was so not good at this femme fatale stuff.

Ronan's megawatt smile was back. "Great, let's go."

This time when he held out his hand, she stepped up to his side. Her body tingled when his palm lightly touched the small of her back, guiding her out of the building. He led her to a sedan that gleamed in the waning sun. Someone had been through the carwash recently. As he opened the door for her, she smiled her thanks and couldn't help noticing that his pants were a little snugger than they had been.

Well, good. She was glad she wasn't the only one aroused by their brief and chaste contact. "So, where are we going?"

Ronan glanced at her as he maneuvered out of the parking lot. "Do you like seafood?"

Raising her eyebrows, she turned to look at him. "Is that a serious question?"

Ronan shrugged. "Sure. Just because you're raised with something, doesn't mean you develop a liking for it. I'm not a big fan of the boiled dinner, for example."

"Oh, I love corned beef and cabbage."

Ronan grimaced. "I'll be sure to let my Uncle Jack know to put you on the invitation list for dinner next St. Patrick's Day. You can have my portion."

"Hmm. I can't wait." She licked her lips. The little grunt that passed his lips told her she'd hit her mark. "Anyway, in answer to your question, yes, I love seafood, especially shellfish."

"Good to hear because I am jonesin' for lobster. And given the balmy night, I thought we'd go to a little place I know up in Rockport." As he said it, she realized he was heading to Route 93 north. "If you don't mind the drive."

"I don't mind. I enjoy riding in the car when I'm not the one driving. I'm like a dog that way," she added with a laugh.

"A dog is not what comes to mind when I think of you, Cassidy."

She laughed again. "I guess that's good to hear. Still, if I were a dog, what kind of dog would I be, do you suppose?"

He looked at her skeptically. "Is this like a Barbara Walters interview?"

"Sure, why not? We can get to know each other by asking silly questions."

"Okay, I'll play along." He hummed for a few seconds as he contemplated his answer. "I guess you'd be a poodle."

"A poodle, why? I don't have curly hair."

"True, but poodles are very smart dogs."

"Oh, I like that. They're often pampered, too, though."

"I wouldn't mind pampering you if you were my poodle. In fact, I'll amend my choice by saying that you would be a teacup poodle." He glanced at her slyly and with enough heat in the brief gaze to make her reach for the vent and turn it to blow directly on her face.

"Really?" she choked out.

"Yup, I'd keep you curled up on my lap." He shot her a wicked smile. Her only response was a sharp exhalation of breath. "Your turn."

Well, Jesus, how was she going to top that little sexual innuendo? She racked her brains for a breed that fit the sexy charmer. Try as she might, though, nothing fit to her satisfaction until she thought outside the box. "You're not a dog at all."

"No?"

"No. You're a cat. Not a house cat, a big cat, like a panther. Sleek and cunning and able to sneak up on your prey and pounce before they even know you're there."

Ronan was silent for long seconds. Finally, he cleared his throat. "I don't think we should play this game anymore. My pants are uncomfortable as it is, frankly, and I really would like to get to Rockport in one piece. What was residency like?"

Cassidy couldn't keep the smile off her face. She liked making a man squirm. Who knew dating could be so much fun? She took pity on him, though, and launched into the ins and outs of medical training. He listened to her, too. She could tell because he interrupted every once in a while, asking relevant questions. There was something very attractive about a man who listened.

Before she knew it, he pulled into the crushed stone parking lot of a small restaurant. It was quaint and a bit crowded, which meant the food was probably good. The hostess greeted Ronan warmly, as if he was well known to the place. So far everyone she saw with him seemed to know and like him. He was that kind of guy. The hostess found a table for them in a corner of the open veranda and handed them simple one page laminated menus.

"I'm having a two pound boiled lobster with a side of potato salad," Ronan said without even looking at the menu. "How about you?"

Cassidy shrugged. "Sounds good to me."

The server arrived to take their drink orders. Ronan went with beer, but Cassidy wanted a clear head, so she asked for iced tea. They ordered their food, too, as they'd already decided. Now that they were face-to-face, she felt a little awkward. Before Ronan could pick up the conversational ball, however, she decided that he'd heard enough about her and wanted to hear more about him. "Tell me about your family."

Ronan's expression became guarded for a second before the easy smile came back. "Not much to tell. I have one older brother and one younger one, both cops, although Finn's badge is still shiny new." He paused when their drinks arrived, then continued. "You may have heard that our parents were murdered eight years ago."

Stunned at the news, Cassidy blinked back at him, trying to dredge up the social niceties that had been drilled into her by her mother. Instead, she blurted out, "That's horrible!"

Ronan took a long swallow of beer. "Yeah, it was and it is. It's still unsolved."

"I would think the police would have worked overtime to find who'd killed one of their own."

"You'd think, yeah. The thing is, my parents were barely in the ground before the rumors started that my father had been dirty and was killed when he tried to double-cross the mobsters who were paying him."

Cassidy frowned. "On what basis was that believed?"

"Good question. You know how rumors are. No one knows where they start, or at least no one owns up to it. But they spread like wildfire, and I can't say no one looked for the killer. They just didn't look very hard, in my estimation." He looked straight at her, and she could see the pain in his eyes. "Anyway, I moved back home to help raise Finn. Now that he's all grown up, I'm free to pursue other pleasures, like having dinner with you."

Just like that, the pain was gone and the seductiveness was back. Their dinners arrived shortly after that, and they both concentrated on cracking open their lobsters. Cassidy allowed the server to tie her plastic bib around her.

Ronan just sneered when offered his. "Lobster bibs are for wimps."

"I don't want to get my dress messy," Cassidy said defensively.

Ronan dipped a piece of claw meat in the drawn butter and popped the dripping morsel into his mouth. When he'd swallowed, he said, "Messy can be fun, Cassidy."

He slowly licked the butter off his lower lip. Her gaze followed his tongue's journey, and her pussy pulsed in response. Okay, that was payback for her cat comment. Still, she was nothing if not competitive.

Leaning over her dinner, she pitched her voice low. "I'm not convinced. You'll have to show me later."

Ronan paused in the middle of cracking a second claw. His gaze scorched her from across the table. "It will be my pleasure."

Dinner was a hurried affair. Lobster shells clattered on their plates as they tore through the barriers and picked out the meat. Each time they put buttery meat into their respective mouths, they exaggerated their movements more and more. They tried to outdo one another in sexualizing their eating, until it got so comical they laughed in between bites. As playful as it was, there was an undercurrent of strong sexual arousal.

They left the restaurant, once Ronan paid the check, holding hands. Back at the car, Ronan unlocked the door by remote and whirled Cassidy so that she was backed against her door.

His kiss came with no further warning, a fervent coupling of their lips that had been fueled by their play at dinner. His arms encircled her waist, and he pressed against her. She could feel how hard he was through the thin fabric of his slacks and her dress. She grabbed his arms and swiveled her hips to rub against him. They both groaned at the friction and used their tongues as surrogates for cock and cunt, thrusting and twining until they had to break apart or pass out from lack of breath.

"Your place or mine?" Ronan asked between gulps.

Cassidy gave a second or two of thought and went with the answer that made her the most comfortable. "Mine, please."

"Yes, ma'am."

Ronan whirled her around and practically shoved her into the car once he had the door open. There were no more playful interviews or questions as he raced down the highway back to Boston. He broke the silence to ask her address and merely raised his eyebrows when she gave it. He raised them again when she directed him to her two car garage, an unheard of luxury for the Back Bay.

She let them into the foyer and gasped when he grabbed her from behind and dove in for another kiss. They fumbled their way up the first two set of stairs before he brought them to a halt. "Mind if I act out a fantasy of mine?"

She looked up at him, all but breathless and hungry for more. "Go for it."

He tugged her into her kitchen and hoisted her onto the counter of her prep island. His obvious strength sent a primitive thrill through her. No man had ever lifted her before Diego and now Ronan. But, no, she wasn't going to think about the other man tonight. She was with Ronan, exactly who she wanted to be with at the moment. The feel of his hands heated her up, while the cool of the granite filtered through the cotton of her dress.

Ronan didn't let her get comfortable or allow rational thought to stay in her head. He skimmed his hands up her thighs as he closed in for another kiss. The way his lips and tongue claimed her, she barely realized he had hooked his fingers in her panties and was tugging them down. She squealed in surprise when his hands returned to her hips and tipped her back. She shot her hands out behind her for balance as he trailed wet kisses down her throat. Instead of giving her aching breasts some attention, he kneeled in front of her.

With her eyelids already at half-mast, she watched him, not understanding what he was up to until he began to kiss her again. This time his lips and tongue worked their way up her inner thigh. She gasped and shuddered when he reached the sensitive taut flesh where leg met hip. Oh, God, she'd never known that tucked away spot could cause her whole body to spasm with pleasure.

Ronan grinned at her reaction, then did the same on the other side. This time when he reached the top, he looked up at her from under his lashes. There was a wicked gleam in his eyes that confirmed she'd been right. He was a cat, and she was his prey, trapped within his embrace and about to be—eaten? Good lord, his tongue laved up her slit in one long stroke. Her body convulsed, her hips thrusting up. She scrambled to grip the smooth surface of the countertop. Her arms shook with her effort to stay upright.

Slipping his arms underneath her thighs, Ronan slid her closer to the counter's edge. His tongue ravaged her clit and the folds around it, driving her wild by constantly changing his strokes to circles and back again. He went from slow laps to fast flicks, and when his lips clasped onto her clit and sucked, she screamed with her release. With her head thrown back and her eyes shut tight, she rode the wave of climax, and still Ronan kept up his assault. She peaked again before she could even catch her breath. Her pussy clenched in a desperate need to hold onto something that wasn't yet there, and her legs squeezed against his hold.

Unable to keep herself upright, Cassidy slid supine onto the counter, her chest heaving with the gasps that came from the strong aftershocks of her orgasm. Ronan had finally taken his mouth away. Her legs flopped down to dangle when he released them. Thank God he'd had his fill. She needed time to recover because she didn't think she could handle coming again so soon. She was wrong.

Ronan's cock slid into her with one fast thrust. Cassidy was coming again before he even hilted himself. Arching her back, she cried out. "Son of a bitch!"

Ronan stilled. "Too much?"

"Don't stop!" Her cunt was delighted to have

something to grasp and squeeze. "Yes," she yelled out her encouragement and pulled him in tighter with her legs when he began to thrust.

Ronan fought to rein himself in. His hands, slick with sweat, gripped Cassidy's thighs tight enough he was afraid he'd leave marks. His dick, happy to finally be where it had demanded to be all night, urged him to pump faster. He might have been capable of controlling himself, but the way Cassidy's cunt sucked him in while her heels drove his ass like a pile driver gave him little choice. Holy shit, she was the most responsive women he'd ever met, coming so fast and so hard, he felt like a super lover.

And she was doing it again, the walls of her pussy closing like a vice and her whole body shaking with her orgasm. The keening cries coming from her mouth sent a shiver of excitement up his spine all on their own. He was doing this to her, making her come and come again. This was number four, or was it five? Fuck if he knew, and it snapped what little control he'd held onto.

With a final thrust balls deep inside her, he exploded. His cock jerked and pulsed its way over the crest. He pressed his body tight against hers, some primitive part of him trying to send his seed deep inside. Too bad for his lizard brain because he'd held it together mentally enough to slide a condom on before he entered her. Still, as he stood there between her legs with his eyes closed, he knew a moment of bliss and could have stayed there all night.

"This was a mistake."

Cassidy's words were like a punch to his gut. His eyes flew open, and he stared down at her. Despite what she'd said, she was lying against the counter with her arms outstretched and a satisfied smile on her lips.

With a slight flutter of her lids, she opened her eyes, and her smile widened as she looked up at him. "We should have done this in my bed. I'll never be able to get up. I'm going to have to sleep here."

Relief flooded through him as the full meaning of her words sank in. He placed a gentle kiss on the inside of her knee and was gratified when her body rippled in response. "Don't worry about a thing. I'll get you where you need to be, sweetheart."

"I think you've already done that, thank you very much. If you can get me up to bed, however, I will be eternally grateful."

With another quick kiss to her leg, he carefully pulled out and disposed of the condom in a nearby bathroom. He couldn't help but notice that Cassidy had a beautiful and expensive home. Family money, obviously. It gave him a typical masculine sense of insecurity for about two seconds before he dismissed it. There was no sense in getting ahead of himself. Right now, he had a beautiful woman laid out in the kitchen like a sushi platter, who needed him to get her tucked in for the night.

Of course that train of thought stirred his cock into thinking maybe it could be tucked in for the night, too.

Knock it off.

He'd worn the woman out, and while he could easily see her rallying at some point later, he didn't want to outwear her, or his welcome.

Returning to the kitchen, he found her right where he'd left her. With a little tugging and sliding, he managed to get her into his arms. The hand cradling her legs brushed against her soft ass and bad thoughts reared up again. No, he was sticking with the plan.

Cassidy curled up against him, her trust that he had her and would safely deliver her to her bed caused his chest to swell. He couldn't resist the temptation to kiss the top of her head. She snuggled closer and giggled. "If I'm the dog and you're the cat," she said in a sleepy voice. "How come I'm the one who feels like purring?"

In way of an answer, he hugged her more tightly as he carried her up the stairs.

****

Diego wanted to smack the well-fucked look off Ronan's face as soon as he saw it, then reminded himself that Ronan had shown more restraint the previous morning. Diego was sure he'd worn the same expression. After a night with Cassidy, what man wouldn't? Jealousy reared up, too, and he shoved it back down. He'd been on one date with the woman and, sex notwithstanding, one date did not a relationship make.

Fortunately, the same could be said for his partner. Cassidy Barnes was a free agent, and he intended to court her as fiercely as he could. He might not be above using dirty tricks where Ronan was concerned, but he would win Cassidy over with romance and sincere desire and interest.

"Good morning," he said pointedly as Ronan hadn't yet seen him.

"Hmm? Oh, yeah, hi." Ronan quickly hid his face behind an enormous container of iced coffee.

Yeah, motherfucker needed the caffeine boost because he hadn't gotten a full night's sleep. Diego shook his head at his own inability to keep the green-eyed monster locked up.

"Any news on your father's old partner?" Best thing was to focus on work.

Ronan slurped on his coffee. Then his gaze shot to a point past Diego's shoulder. "Here comes our answer now."

Diego swiveled his chair around and saw a leggy redhead striding toward them. She looked like hell on wheels and, like his partner, she was sucking on a mega container of caffeine. Hers, however, was black.

"Hey," she said to Ronan when she arrived. She turned to look at Diego. "I'm Regan Malloy."

He stood and shook her hand. "Diego Nieves."

"The New York transplant," she stated simply, although the once-over she gave him made him want to stand up straighter. "I won't hold your previous city against you given that you made the right decision to come here." She paused. "Regardless of the reason."

Diego tensed and waited for her to say more. She'd obviously learned about the shooting somehow, maybe by just doing an internet search. God knows his name was plastered all over the tabloids. Why she would have bothered to check was a mystery because not even Ronan seemed to care why he'd transferred.

"Family looks out for family, you know?" was all she said in further explanation.

"Is there something I'm missing?" Ronan asked.

Regan patted his shoulder patronizingly. "Nothing you need to worry your pretty little head about, cousin."

Okay, she was another Callaghan of some degree. When she didn't say anything else, Diego sat back down.

"So," Ronan said. "Uncle Connor?"

Regan sneered down at him. "You're twenty-six

fucking years old, Ronan. You can call him just Connor now."

Ronan shrugged. "Habit."

With a sigh and a roll of her eyes at Diego, she said, "Pops said the guy's up at his cabin on Moosehead Lake for vacation and will be for another few days. The good news is that Pops invited him to his birthday bash. He's turning sixty-five, and we're having a big barbeque for him on Sunday," she explained to Diego. "He and Connor used to be pretty good friends back in the day, so his inviting him isn't surprising."

"Huh," Ronan interjected. "I hate the idea of waiting. Maybe we should take a drive up there."

"Seriously? That's like a six hour drive one way, plus you have to find him and I'm not sure if anyone has an exact address for him." Regan sucked deeply on her coffee. "That is, if they even have addresses way the fuck up there."

"We have other leads to follow," Diego offered. "We haven't sifted through all the paper we found at Seamus' apartment, and the tech guys are still going through his computer. Plus, we have known associates from his file. We have stuff to do that might solve the case."

Ronan didn't look convinced. "I've got this itch between my shoulder blades telling me the answer to this murder is imbedded in the past."

Regan placed her hand on his shoulder again, this time in a comforting gesture. "It's tempting to think so, I know, but it's long odds."

Her cousin looked as if he were about to argue with her, then his shoulders slumped. "Yeah, I know you're probably right. We won't disturb the guy on his vacation." He shot a look at Diego. "You're coming to the barbeque so we can talk to him as soon as he returns."

"I shouldn't. It's a family thing. We can talk to him after." Diego looked at Regan for back up.

She shook her head. "Nope, Ronan's right. Come to the party and drag him off to a corner at some point. Pops won't mind. Hell, it will give him a kick to continue to help with the investigation."

Diego knew when to give up gracefully. "Fine, if you insist. What does the birthday boy want?"

"No presents," Regan said.

"My mother would box my ears if she knew I'd gone to someone's house, let alone a birthday party, empty handed. He must like to get something."

"Jameson," the cousins said in unison.

"Of course." Diego shook his head and smiled indulgently.

"See you around, cousin. Nice meeting you, Diego."

The two men watched Regan walk away. She did make an enticing sight, with long, lean legs and a high tight ass. Diego's interests, however, were already occupied elsewhere.

"She's single, you know."

"Nice try." Diego swung his chair around to look Ronan in the eye. "I like Cassidy. I mean I *really* like her."

Ronan stared back at him, sucking on his coffee for a minute. "Then we have a problem because I *really* like her, too. She and I went out last night."

Diego fought to keep the exasperation out of his voice. "I know."

Leaning forward, Ronan said, "It wasn't a pity date, either, like she was too polite to cancel on me after going out with you."

When Ronan didn't say anything further, Diego understood what wasn't being said. Shit, Cassidy had slept with Ronan. While Diego had barely known her for more than a day, he was a good judge of character. He was sure she wasn't the kind of woman that strung guys along or got some sick thrill from playing guys off each other. He could be wrong, of course, but he didn't think so. Besides, if she were, then both he and Ronan were being played as chumps. Although, he'd known his partner only slightly longer than he had Cassidy, he didn't think Ronan was the kind of guy who could be manipulated by a woman any more than Diego was.

He huffed out a breath. "I get it. So what's that supposed to mean? You expect me to back off or something?"

Ronan cocked his head, an expression on his face that Diego couldn't quite read, yet made him want to smack the guy anyway. "You don't strike me as the backing-off type. I think it's only fair to warn you, though, that I'm not either. In fact, I have another date with Cassidy tomorrow night."

Fuck! Diego'd been trying to play it cool with Cassidy, not be overbearing, so he'd left things a bit vague with her about when they'd go out again. Being the gentleman had obviously been a sucker move. Still, there was perhaps a window of opportunity. "Not tonight?"

"Nah, she's got some girls' night out work thing tonight."

Okay, fine. That left Friday open. Pulling out his

phone, he swiveled away from Ronan and shot a message off to Cassidy. *Thinking of you,* querida. *Are you free Friday night?*

He plastered a pleasant smile on his face as he turned and found Ronan glaring at him. But his partner didn't say anything, which was just as well because they really did have a job to do, a murder to solve, even if O'Malley was some low-life creep who may or may not have had anything to do with the Callaghan murders.

Ronan stood abruptly, his coffee clenched in his hand. "Let's go bug the tech guys. I want to know what was on O'Malley's computer."

Diego stood as well. "Okay, but don't they notify you as soon as they're done?"

"Yeah. I like to bug them anyway."

Diego wasn't so sure that was a productive strategy. He'd learned in New York that the more you pestered the tech guys, the more they seemed to slow down just out of perverseness. He tagged along behind his partner nevertheless. From what little he'd observed about Ronan, he seemed to know a lot of people in the department by name, a real hail-fellow-well-met kind of guy. He was probably good at charming things out of others, especially women.

That thought led to Cassidy. He pulled his phone out of his pocket and took a surreptitious look. He couldn't hold back the grin when he saw she'd replied.

Yes, I am. My choice on date venue?

Whatever you want. He texted back and pocketed the phone as they entered the elevator.

Ronan eyed him suspiciously. "You look happy all of a sudden."

"Do I?"

Diego shrugged. He wasn't going to tease the other guy about his new plans with Cassidy. Not only didn't he want to escalate an already difficult situation, it also would be disrespectful to the lady involved. She wasn't a pawn in a game between the two men, nor was she some prize to be fought over. He'd been serious when he'd told Ronan that he liked her. He hadn't had a girlfriend in nearly two years, and dating for the last nine months had been out of the question. The stress and depression over the shooting had left nothing in him for any kind of intimate relationship.

They travelled to the forensics department in silence, the only sound being their footsteps and Ronan's occasional slurp of his coffee. Jesus, didn't the guy go anywhere without a drink in his hand? Diego was surprised when Ronan approached a young man instead of a woman. He'd been sure his partner was going to flatter someone out of information.

The tech guy was dark skinned with closely cropped hair and horn-rimmed glasses. He looked as if he were trying to epitomize the nerd stereotype. His eyes went wide when he saw Ronan. "Aw, for God's sake, Callaghan, you have the patience of a two-year old."

Ronan flashed a bright smile. "Come on, Frankie, you know you love it when I visit you." Slipping his hand into his pocket, he pulled out what appeared to be a couple of tickets, although for what, Diego couldn't tell. Ronan handed them quietly over to Frankie, who shoved them into his own pocket.

He grinned widely. "Maybe I do." He nodded at Diego. "You got stuck with this guy, huh?"

Diego shrugged. "I'm new to the force and beggars can't be choosers."

Frankie chuckled and Ronan sneered at both of them. "What've you got for us?"

The computer specialist took over Frankie's demeanor, and he swiveled his attention back to the netbook he'd been checking.

"I don't have much for you, I'm afraid. The guy had a serious porn habit, I can tell you that much." Frankie shuddered. "I've been wading through smut for hours, and as near as I can tell, his tastes devolved into the more bizarre over the years. So far, though, there's nothing imbedded in the videos other than the porn itself."

"I wouldn't expect there to be," Ronan said. "The guy doesn't strike me as being the brainy type. What about email?"

"Other than booking appointments with various escort services, there's not much there. If he had any friends, they weren't the type to correspond."

"Huh," Diego and Ronan said it together, then glanced at each other warily. It was way too soon in their partnership to start talking and acting alike.

Patting Frankie on the shoulder, Ronan said, "Thanks, man. I appreciate the update."

"No problem. I'll let you know if I find anything useful."

Diego led the way out of the room. "So, we go back to slogging through the files we have and start canvassing his old associates. Maybe we'll get lucky like we did with his sister."

"Maybe." Ronan didn't look convinced, and Diego understood his partner was really hoping that the interview with his father's old partner on Sunday would produce better results.

Diego sincerely hoped they'd catch a break somehow, and that it would lead to the solving of the Callaghan murders.

Chapter Five

"Let me get this straight, you've gone from dating no one to dating two guys at once?"

Gina, one of the morgue technicians stared at Cassidy a bit glassy-eyed. The others had gotten off work earlier than Cassidy had, which meant they'd had a head start with the cocktails. Because she was on her second dirty martini and was fairly bursting with the need to discuss her dating situation with someone, her double romance was now on the table for discussion.

"Yes, that is correct," she replied, then took a sip of her drink. "And they're partners."

"Who are we talking about?" This was from Keisha, another medical examiner.

Cassidy hesitated to name names, then figured why the hell not? "Ronan Callaghan and Diego Nieves."

The other two women reared back on a communal gasp. "Ronan Callaghan is a hottie!" Gina exclaimed in a too loud voice. She immediately shushed herself. "All the Callaghan brothers are hot. And Ronan could charm the birds out of the trees."

"Well, he certainly charmed me out of the morgue." *And, into bed.*

"I don't know this other guy, though," Keisha said, popping a pretzel into her mouth.

"He's new, like brand spanking new this week." Gina apparently was wired into the force's gossip. "I saw him the other day when they were in." She made an O out of her mouth and groaned. "Gives the Callaghan brothers a run for their money. Looks super sweet, too."

Cassidy smiled. "He is sweet and romantic." Plus, he had a wild side given his bike that was especially appealing because it was so unexpected of him.

"And you've got both of these guys sniffing around?" Keisha asked, swirling her drink. "Girl, that is so not fair."

"I know," Cassidy replied with a sigh. "I don't know how it happened, but I couldn't say no to either of them. I still can't. I have a date with Ronan tomorrow and one with Diego on Friday."

"Wow, talk about a full dance card." Gina tipped the rest of her drink in her mouth, then motioned to the server for another round.

"Yeah." Cassidy tried to finish her drink with the same ease as her companion and only managed to choke herself on the strong liquor. When she'd finished coughing, she wiped her mouth and frowned.

"The thing is, I like both of them equally. I probably should choose between them, though."

Keisha slapped her empty glass down. "Why would you do that?"

"I'm not sure it's fair to them."

"Why not?"

"Yeah, why not?" Gina demanded, too, then smiled brightly as their server, Todd according to his name tag, placed new drinks in front of them. "What do you think, Todd?"

"Gina!" Cassidy was mortified when the young man looked back and forth between them.

"What do I think about what?" he asked as he

cleaned up their table.

"Cassidy here thinks she shouldn't be dating two men at once, that it's not fair to them and she should choose."

Todd shrugged. "Seems fine to me. If I were you," he added with a knowing look directed at Cassidy, "I'd even date them on the same night and fuck them at the same time." With a wink, he left.

Keisha and Gina whooped at the suggestion. Cassidy sat there with her mouth open. "I am so not doing that." This time when she slammed her drink back, she didn't cough one bit.

****

Cassidy was still not willing to take the advice of Todd the Drink Server, who was possibly gay and definitely sexually adventurous. Even so, she found herself in the weird position of riding in a car with both Ronan and Diego. Ronan was driving and Diego was sitting in the back, a place he didn't want to be, but there was no way the three of them could fit in the front seat. Likewise, Diego's Harley was out of the question. She could have driven, although it seemed silly for her to drive Ronan to his old neighborhood, and unless both guys sat in the back like a pair of male Miss Daisies while she chauffeured, it wasn't going to fix the seating problem anyway.

How had she landed in this awkward situation? After a night of soul-searching with her friends, fueled unhelpfully by lots of alcohol, she'd gone out with Ronan, then Diego again, then Ronan yet again. On all three occasions, she'd had a wonderful meal followed by fantastic sex. Yes, her pussy was feeling tender and her nipples likewise had tucked themselves up for a day of rest. And yet, when she thought of how each of these two men made her feel, her body throbbed with anticipation and eagerness. Being cooped up in a car with them did nothing to calm her down, that was for sure.

The idea of her coming to his uncle's birthday party had been Ronan's although Diego had seconded the motion once she'd told him of it. It was technically Diego's day if you counted that she was alternating days between them. The marathon of dating was not only beyond her previous experience, she never would have imagined such a thing in her wildest dreams. She'd fallen into the rhythm of it naturally, though, and it felt right.

So it was Diego's day, but he had to come to the party to question someone who was going to be here about the murder they were investigating. She wasn't sure exactly what was going on and, being the medical examiner and not a detective, didn't feel she had the right to ask for details. It was enough that Diego wanted to spend the time with her so much he'd share her company with Ronan. It was all perfectly civilized if one discounted the palpable tension between the two men. She breathed a quiet sigh of relief when Ronan pulled up behind another car against the curb on a quiet Charlestown street.

"My uncle's house is the green two-family down there," he pointed out.

They all exited the car, Cassidy and Diego carrying their respective gifts for the birthday boy, whom Cassidy wouldn't know if she tripped over him. They walked down the sidewalk. It was a tight fit, but the guys managed to flank her so they walked three abreast.

It was kind of thrilling to have two gorgeous men accompany her, although she wondered what the Callaghans would think of it all. A three-way date was not the norm.

As they reached the walkway leading up to the house, a teenage boy stomped by them. With his hands shoved into the pockets of his jeans and his shoulders slouched, the kid's emotional state was obvious. He wasn't looking forward to hot dogs and cake, apparently.

"Hey, Craig," Ronan called out.

The kid barely grunted in response and kept going around the side of the house. Two men came walking up, holding hands and wearing their own scowls. Cassidy could tell immediately that the younger of the two was a Callaghan.

"Sorry about that," the guy said. "Craig wanted to stay home and play video games, like he doesn't get to do that every day."

Ronan smacked him on the shoulder. "Oh, I'm so loving this, little brother. Now you know what it was like for me when you were that age."

"Yeah, yeah." The guy's scowl disappeared when he looked at Cassidy. "Hi, sorry, for the mini-drama. I'm Finn Callaghan, and this is my partner, Michael Caruso. The kid that nearly ran you down is our foster son, Craig."

Ronan made the necessary introductions, and when they'd all shaken hands and exchanged greetings, they followed the trail laid by the sullen Craig into the backyard. There were dozens of people already hanging around, drinking, playing, and laughing. Cassidy paused a second, feeling a bit intimidated. Diego placed a reassuring hand on the small of her back.

"I don't know anyone, either. We'll stick together."

Grabbing her hand, Ronan said, "Yes, we will. Let me introduce you to my uncle."

The three of them walked through the yard stuck together, as if they were part of the road company for The Golden Goose. Cassidy didn't mind too much as she felt safe and comfortable with each of these men. The way they touched her was both arousing and strangely cozy. Once again, she wondered how they must look to Ronan's family and friends. No one gave them any funny looks, at least not that she could tell. Perhaps she was being overly sensitive. Of course, *she* knew how weird it was for them to attend as a troika because she knew how intimate she and each of the men had become. She really hoped that closeness wasn't being telegraphed by her or the guys.

Ronan led them over to a place under a large shady tree. An older man with grizzled features and buzzed white hair held court in a wheelchair. The birthday boy, no doubt. A rather stunning and tall redhead stood next to him, her hand on one of the chair's steering handles. Ronan had told her he had a female cousin who was a homicide detective. This had to be her.

The woman smiled broadly when she caught sight of Ronan. "Hey, there, cousin."

The birthday boy waved at someone before turning to them, his shrewd eyes taking them all at a glance. He wrinkled his brow, as if working out a hard puzzle. Okay, so this guy had definitely seen the oddity in their threesome. Yet all he did was smile as widely as the woman beside him. He held out his hand when Ronan stepped up.

"Good of you to come, boyo." There was a slight Irish lilt to his voice that sounded like he'd emigrated and not been born in Boston.

Ronan not only clasped the hand, he leaned in to kiss the older man loudly on the forehead. "Like I'd miss it."

He gently pulled Cassidy in closer as he hadn't let her hand go when he greeted his uncle. Diego, of course, kept his palm plastered to the small of her back.

"Uncle Jack, Regan, meet Dr. Cassidy Barnes, the new medical examiner. And this is my new partner, Diego Nieves."

With her right hand held hostage by Ronan, all she could do was nod and smile. "It's nice to meet you both. Thank you for having us."

Hmm, where did the *us* come from? It's seemed natural to say it, and she was hard pressed to say whether she meant us as in her and Diego or us as in her, Diego, and Ronan. And why did the latter feel so right?

"We're delighted to have you," Jack said. His sincerity was obvious. If he thought it was strange that his nephew came with two dates, he didn't hint as much.

Regan, however, had other ideas. Her gaze darted back and forth between Diego and Ronan before it landed on Cassidy. "I've heard of you, but so far haven't had an opportunity to stand over a DB with you. I can see that, as usual, my cousin has worked fast." She directed a smirk at Ronan.

Not knowing what to say to that observation, Cassidy fell back on the kind of social politeness drilled into her since childhood. She held out the party bag in her left hand. "I'm sorry, Mr. Malloy, I didn't get the memo about your drinking preferences. This is wine, not whisky."

Reaching for her offering, Jack smiled up at her. "Not to worry, my girl here likes to take part in the grape." He handed the bag over to Regan who lost no time opening it. She looked at the label and gave a nod of approval. "And it's Jack, please. We don't stand on ceremony in this part of Boston."

Cassidy didn't imagine in the least that it was a subtle dig at her more upscale neighborhood, and even if it had been, it would have been well-founded. Regardless, Ronan squeezed her hand. She looked up and gave him a reassuring smile. She liked his uncle and his cousin already. She couldn't possibly take offense at anything they said.

Diego stepped forward, his hand still touching her. "I did get the memo, sir." Grinning, he handed over his bag and was rewarded when Jack smacked his lips.

"I do love my Jameson. Thanks, and the same goes—it's Jack. Put this with the other gifts, won't you, sweetheart?" he asked, giving it to his daughter.

"Sure, Pops."

Jack's expression turned abruptly sober. "Connor's not here yet, but he promised he'd stop by at some point even though he's just getting back from vacation."

"Thanks, Uncle Jack, I appreciate it."

The older man turned pensive. "I hope he has some answers. I always felt he knew more than he let on years ago."

While he didn't come out and say so, Cassidy understood the veiled reference was to the murder of Ronan's parents. Ronan stiffened a bit beside her, so it was her turn to squeeze his hand. Although she didn't know what was going on, she wanted to reassure him that she was here if he needed her.

"It's probably a long shot for him to help us with the current investigation, but nothing else has panned out so far."

"Well," Regan interjected with a note of lightness in her tone. "In the meantime, how about a beer? There's plenty of nibblies laid out, and Aunt Mary is taking orders for burgers or dogs."

"Do you have any Sam Adams?" Diego asked. "I've been meaning to try it."

Regan gave him a pitying look. "Christ Jesus, you'd think New York was on the other side of the world. Come on, then."

Cassidy, Diego, and Ronan turned as one, and with her left hand free, somehow it had ended up clasped by Diego. Now they really did look ridiculous, and she wondered how she was supposed to eat and drink. An image of the men feeding her with their own hands popped into her head. She stumbled a bit as the fantasy grabbed her right between her legs. Each man closed in to make sure she was stable. She flashed them a weak smile. This was going to be a long afternoon.

****

Ronan wasn't surprised when his brothers came to sit on either side of him. He was surprised they'd managed to wait until lunch was mostly consumed before cornering him. Of course, he'd been staying close to Cassidy for the entire afternoon. It wasn't until his female relatives wrangled her away for hen talk while they fussed over his cousin Siobhan's new baby girl that he'd been vulnerable for attack. With Diego engrossed in a Red Sox vs. Yankee's discussion with Uncle Jack and his coterie of retirees, Ronan was wide open. Daire and Finn didn't even bother to say anything at first, they simply sat and stared at him.

Ronan sighed. "What?"

Clasping a hand on Ronan's shoulder, Daire said, "I get the gorgeous medical examiner, but your partner doesn't strike me as your type. He's a little, too, I don't know—male?" He leaned over Ronan's front to get confirmation from Finn.

Their little brother didn't hesitate to join in the fun. "Yeah, that was what I thought, too." Finn nudged Ronan. "Are you switching over to my team, bro?"

"Ha, ha." Ronan didn't bother to glare at either of them. His attention remained fixed on Cassidy. Someone said something to make her laugh. The way she looked as she threw back her head with her lips parted hit him not just in his balls, but somewhere much farther north. God, she was so lovely and delightful.

He wasn't the only one to notice, however. Diego's gaze was also fixed on her even as he spoke with Jack and the others. The knowledge spiked his blood pressure in a whole different way. God, he'd never been the jealous type, always pulling out when he had competition. This was different, though. He wasn't going to give up Cassidy without a fight, even though it meant fighting with his own partner.

A hand waved in front of his face. "Seriously, Ronan, what the fuck is going on?"

"Nothing," he lied. When it was clear that answer wasn't going to be accepted, he grudgingly added more. "Cassidy and I are dating, that's true. I thought it might be fun to bring her. Nieves and I are waiting for Dad's old partner to show up because he might tie in with a murder investigation we've got going. We want to ask him a few questions."

Mention of their father took his brothers' focus off Cassidy as he knew it would.

"Do you mean the homeless guy found by the Charles last week?" Daire asked, his teasing tone gone.

"Yeah, except we don't think he was homeless. He had a place he was renting for years still available, and other than his clothing, he didn't look like someone who'd been living on the streets. We think the whole thing was staged."

"Why would anyone bother?" This from Finn, who, like Daire, was all business.

"That's the sixty-four thousand dollar question. The vic was a snitch of Dad's, and he's been living off the grid if not on the streets for about eight years." Both of his brothers swore. "Yeah, I know. It's easy to read into it as being relevant." He shrugged. "We'll see. I find it odd that this low-level snitch came into enough money to live comfortably all of these years."

Finn leaned in closer. "You think he sold Dad out?"

"Or pulled the trigger?" Daire added.

Ronan shook his head slowly and shot a reassuring grin over to Cassidy when she glanced his way. "I don't know. He wasn't a hard-core criminal, no convictions for violent offenses, but selling people out was his stock in trade."

The three of them were quiet for a while as they pondered the possibilities. Ronan's attention was divided at best, however. He couldn't keep from tracking Cassidy's every move. He liked the way she looked sitting among his female relatives. They all seemed to like her, Regan included, and that made her even more appealing to him. Family meant the world to him. Naturally, his brothers finished digesting his news about O'Malley and circled back to the original topic.

"You do know that Nieves has a thing for her, too, right?" Daire asked.

Ronan made a face. "Yeah, I do know that. He's been dating her as well."

Finn whistled. "Wow, and I thought meeting my partner while posing as an underage prostitute was a weird how-I-met-your-mother kind of story."

"It's not like that. Cassidy and I are just hanging out, having fun. We've known each other for less than a week. Diego, the fucker," he said before he could censor himself, "asked her out after I did, although he managed to get his date with her in first."

Daire chuckled. "You must be getting old, little brother. I've never known another man to outflank you before."

"Bite me."

"I'm confused," Finn interjected before Daire could respond. "How's this working today with the three of you out together? It's like a double date minus another woman. Are you all going home together or something?"

The question surprised and maybe even shocked Ronan so much he tore his gaze away from Cassidy. "What the hell kind of question is that?"

Finn shrugged. "No judgment implied. Look at me and Michael. Lots of people are shocked at the idea of two men."

"Troglodytes, maybe." Ronan hated the fact that

there were people in the world who judged his brother harshly for being who he was.

Finn grinned. "Maybe, but my point is, you need to do what works best for you so long as you're not hurting anybody."

Ronan shifted his focus back to Cassidy. Although what his brother was suggesting might sound plausible in the abstract, he had a feeling it would hurt the woman in the center of the matter. He knew he wasn't good at sharing anything, let alone something as important as a woman he cared for.

He glanced over at his partner. What he didn't know about Diego would fill Fenway Park. He was willing to bet, however, that his partner was not the kind of guy who played well with others either.

"Hey." Daire nudged Ronan. "Uncle Conner has arrived."

Thoughts of Cassidy and threesomes fled as Ronan traced his brother's line of vision and saw their father's old partner saunter into the backyard. It had been years since he'd seen the man. The image in his head was sorely out of date. Connor Mahurin was past middle-age, as white haired as the older Jack and moving slowly enough to imply his body gave him trouble. The pot belly he sported certainly wasn't a sign of health, and even from a distance, his face looked haggard. It was hard to believe he'd just come back from vacation.

Ronan stood up and didn't spare a word or a glance for his brothers as he moved to intercept the older cop. Diego was likewise watching the man's approach, having apparently figured out who he was, or maybe Jack had told him. In any event, Ronan reached them all just as Connor was shaking Jack's hand.

"Happy birthday, old man," Connor said with the kind of phlegmy voice associated with long-time smokers.

Jack gave him a grudging smile. "Call me old all you want. So long as I'm breathing, it's fine by me. You remember my nephew, Ronan." Jack gave a nod in Ronan's direction.

Connor turned to Ronan with a guarded look. "I do, of course. How've you been?" he asked, extending his hand.

"Well enough, thanks." Ronan noticed the man's palm was ever so sweaty. "This is my partner, Diego Nieves."

Connor gave Diego the same look and hand. "Oh? I thought it was Rory's youngest who was light in the loafers."

Whether it was the casual mention of his father's name or the offensive and out-of-date insult to Finn, or most likely both, Ronan felt his hackles go up. With bared teeth, he took a step forward before a gesture from Jack told him to rein it in. They weren't going to get many answers from Connor if Ronan knocked all of his teeth out.

"I'm his partner on the force," Diego said, helpfully distracting Connor while Ronan pulled his shit together.

Connor chuckled. "Oh, of course. Of course." He gave Diego the once-over. "I didn't realize we had many P.R.s in Boston."

Seriously? It was as if the guy was trying to start a fight. Could he be that gauche, or was he angling to distract them from something else? There was no way he knew they wanted to interview him about O'Malley.

Or was there?

Diego didn't rise to the bait. He stood staring back at the other man with a vague smile on his face. Ronan had to hand it to him. He was a cooler head than Ronan. A few tense seconds ticked by before Jack intervened.

"The boys have something to talk to you about, Connor. I'm going over to have a look at my new grandniece." He gestured to a couple of his friends who'd been hanging nearby, eyes and ears open to the weird interaction. They got the message and helped him steer away.

Connor eyed Ronan and Diego suspiciously. "What do you need to talk to me about? I'm a desk man these days."

"We know, sir." Once again, Diego's ability to shut down any anger he felt was impressive. "We're actually interested in anything you can tell us about an old snitch of yours and Ronan's father's. Seamus O'Malley. Do you remember him?"

Connor's eyes went wide at the mention of the vic's name. Ronan didn't think the guy should ever quit the force and go into acting because he wasn't very convincing.

"Gee, I don't know, fellas. We had lots of snitches back in the day, and Rory was always better at working them than I was. Let me think." With his hand rubbing his chin, he stared at the ground for close to a minute. "I think I do remember the guy, skinny, shifty-eyed, although they kind of all were you know," he added with a hollow chuckle. "A poor boy working the parameter of the mob, not a big fish." As if any snitch ever was high up the chain of command. "Why do you ask?"

"He's dead," Ronan said. "His throat was slit almost a week ago."

Connor spread his arms out. "Well, now that's hardly surprising. Guys like that usually end up killed or spending the rest of their lives in Walpole. He was no Whitey Bulger, if you know what I mean."

Ronan leaned into the guy a bit. "Yeah, the funny thing was, he'd been living on the down-low in West Roxbury since around the time my folks were murdered."

Connor's face morphed into sadness. This expression, at least, looked more genuine. "I don't know what to say. There was nothing in the evidence to suggest O'Malley or any of Rory's snitches had anything to do with the killing. At least, not that I know of. It wasn't my case. I was too close to be let in on the investigation. It was handled by other cops, as you well know."

"And never solved," Ronan bit out.

Diego's hand landed gently on Ronan's arm, whether in comfort or in warning, he wasn't sure.

"Do you remember seeing or hearing anything about O'Malley since that time?" Diego asked.

"No, can't say that I did." Connor shook his head and shrugged. "Sorry, boys, I can't help you."

"Thanks for your time anyway." Curling his fingers around Ronan's arm, Diego walked away, pulling Ronan with him.

Ronan managed to give Connor a brief nod when all he really wanted to do was knock him to the ground and beat information out of him. "He's lying," he hissed to his partner.

"I know," Diego mumbled back. He slowed down

and turned part way to look behind them. "We'll probably find something helpful on O'Malley's laptop," he called out to Connor.

Ronan turned, too, and saw Connor frozen in mid-stride as he moved to leave the yard.

"Laptop, you say?" the older man called out.

"Yeah," Diego replied with a grin. "It's an old beat-up thing filled with porn, but you never know."

With that parting shot, he kept going, and Ronan didn't resist when Diego tugged on his arm once more. They headed over to where Cassidy was now talking to Finn and Michael.

Ronan shook Diego's hand off. "I thought it was a *netbook,* and you just baited him."

"I figure he would understand laptop better, and damn right I did. P.R.? I didn't hear that shit back in New York. What does he think this is West fucking Side fucking Story?"

Ronan couldn't help giving his partner a feral grin. "I like your style, Nieves."

Ronan meant the compliment. Connor was lying through his teeth, and if he was involved with O'Malley's murder, he would sweat the knowledge that he and whoever he was involved with had missed something as potentially important as a computer with incriminating files. Hopefully, it would goad them into doing something stupid, although what that would be, he couldn't say. It was still a good strategy.

Yeah, he liked his new partner just fine. They could be great friends, too, if only the asshole wasn't interested in Cassidy.

****

If there was a word in either English or Spanish

that could describe the day accurately, Diego didn't know it. Spending the afternoon with both Cassidy and Ronan would have been surreal enough. Add in the strange interview with Mahurin that eerily tied eight-year-old murders with a current one, and you had one fuckingly weird day. Except that one disparaging word wasn't going to cut it because he'd enjoyed himself on many levels. The Callaghan/Malloy family was big, boisterous, and welcoming. It reminded him of his own and made him both more and less homesick. He'd appreciated the way he'd been accepted into the Irish clan so readily on the bare fact that he was Ronan's partner.

Being with Cassidy, touching her, talking to her, and just having the pleasure of watching her had been wonderful. The only thing that marred his time with her was the very thing that had made him welcome at the birthday barbeque to begin with—Ronan. His partner was great to work with on the investigation, but a thorn in his side when it came to romancing Cassidy. There had been no chance to spend time with her alone. Of course, he hadn't given Ronan the chance, either, so they were on even ground.

And Diego had to take some comfort in convincing Cassidy to ride in the backseat with him on the way home from the party. She'd ridden with Ronan in the front on the way there, so it was only fair she would switch on the return leg. He didn't care that he'd sounded needy in his request. He wanted to be as close to her, physically and emotionally, as he could. This might be a game to Ronan, but Diego was falling for Cassidy. What little time he'd managed to spend with her had proven to be more important than a casual fling.

She mattered.

He glanced up and caught Ronan staring at them in the rear view mirror as they waited at a red light. The waves of hostility were palpable. Tough shit. Fair was fair, and besides, Cassidy had refused to hold hands with Diego when he'd tried as they drove off from the Malloy house. He supposed she didn't want to fan the flames by giving him a right Ronan couldn't enjoy. Understanding her motive didn't make the smirk Ronan had given him through the damn mirror any easier to swallow.

This time on a Sunday night, it didn't take long to go from working class Charlestown to upscale Back Bay. Ronan double parked in front of Cassidy's brownstone and turned around to face them. Diego could see the question in the man's face, so he beat him to the punch.

"Any chance we can come in for a cup of coffee?" he asked, twisting his body to face her.

Ronan glared at him. "Yeah, I could use some if you don't mind." His face broke out into a big smile that Diego had to admit was the epitome of charm itself. The fucker.

Cassidy's eyes darted back and forth between them, eyes narrowed and wheels turning in her beautiful head. She didn't look particularly happy about the idea. Finally, she sighed. "Okay, sure. Why don't you turn at the next block and you can park in my garage.

"You have a garage?" Diego asked, his eyebrows raised.

"A two-car garage, yes," Cassidy confirmed.

Diego whistled in appreciation as Ronan shifted the

car back into gear. As little as he knew about Boston, Diego understood the fact that she had so much private parking in a location like this must have meant big bucks. His expectation was confirmed when they pulled into the tight space next to a sporty Mercedes.

As the three of them got out of Ronan's car, Diego took a moment to admire Cassidy's wheels. "This is beautiful. Do you get a chance to drive it much?"

"Not really. It's mostly to make it easier to visit my parents and to go to our summer house in Maine." As she said the words, she winced.

"You have a house in Maine?" Ronan asked as he, too, perused her impressive car.

"A family home," she was quick to clarify. She seemed uncomfortable talking about her wealth. "In Kennebunkport."

Diego knew less about Maine than he did Boston, but he remembered that the Bush family had a compound up there. Wow. Even though he could have easily spent the next hour drooling over her car, he didn't like the idea of her being embarrassed or anything. "So, coffee?"

Cassidy rewarded his efforts with a slight smile that didn't entirely reach her eyes. "Right. Come on in."

She led them through a back entrance to her first floor and up to the kitchen level. He hadn't had a chance to see this part of the house the two times he'd been there. Her bedroom had been his choice of destination. He couldn't be sure, but he thought Ronan appeared familiar with the room.

For a few seconds, he couldn't control the images that popped up in his mind about what his partner and Cassidy might have been up to in this place of granite and steel. Jealousy, hot and strong, pumped through his nerves, a thing about himself he hated. There was more, though. Part of his reaction was simply the hotness of the idea. And that was disturbing on so many levels.

Cassidy looked perfect in the beautiful setting of her kitchen. She really was a classy woman and definitely out of his league and Ronan's. Diego's head told him as much, although his body didn't care one bit. Even with the dampening presence of Ronan, Diego's cock twitched in his pants as Cassidy bent over to pull something from under the island. Ronan's watched her as well, a hunger in his eyes that had to match Diego's. He wanted to slap his hand over Ronan's face to stop him. It was a stupid, yet primitive impulse. A low sound passed his lips before he could stop it.

Cassidy popped back up. "Did you say something?"

Ronan shot him a smirk. "Yeah, Diego, did you say something?" His tone implied he knew exactly what had happened.

Clearing his throat, Diego lied smoothly. "Sorry, just a little cough. I have seasonal allergies." Which was true if it had been spring and not the end of summer.

"Oh, well, I was thinking maybe you guys really would prefer wine to coffee given the lateness of the hour." Cassidy held up a bottle of red.

"Sounds good."

"Whatever you want."

The two men talked over each and ended on a mutual glare. With a barely audible sigh, Cassidy opened a drawer and, pulling out a cork screw, opened the bottle with practiced ease. She reached up to take down three glasses from an overhead cupboard. Once again, their eyes followed her. The graceful way she moved was enchanting, and her skinny jeans hugged her sweet ass alluringly. She poured a half glass for each of them and slid them over the island.

"Why don't we go sit in the living room?" She didn't wait for them to reply, picking her own glass up and sashaying out of the room.

Diego and Ronan jostled for position, each trying to be right behind her. It was so juvenile that Diego almost laughed. Almost. The need to keep Ronan from taking Cassidy away from him overrode what little sense he had left. They panted after her like wolves stalking a female in heat. Diego's cock strained against his jeans. He didn't bother to worry about it showing, however. He figured Ronan was in a similar state, and as determined as Diego was to avoid seeing his partner's hard-on, he figured Ronan must feel the same way.

Cassidy didn't so much as glance over her shoulder. She must have understood how things were between her guests, though, because she chose to sit in a winged backed chair, leaving the other chair and the sofa free. Diego was tempted to take the second chair to be closer to her. He picked the sofa instead so that he could look at her full-on. Ronan must have had the same idea given that he elected to slide in next to Diego.

They spent the next couple of minutes sipping their wine in awkward silence. Diego wasn't so sure alcohol was a good idea given his state of mind and body. He drank sparingly, his gaze fixed on Cassidy. She didn't look happy. Slumped against the chair with her legs crossed, she stared pensively at the ground while she toyed with her drink. He wanted to say something, what he didn't know. Out of the corner of his eye, Ronan's mouth opened, then closed without a sound coming out.

Finally, Cassidy broke the silence. "I'm not cut out for this. I thought I was, but I'm not." She looked up at them. "I like you both. I mean I *really* like you both. Do you understand?"

Diego and Ronan both nodded dumbly.

Cassidy's chest rose on a deep breath she let out as another sigh, this one louder than the one in the kitchen. "I thought I could date both of you, sleep with both of you, and somehow it would be okay. It's not. I look at the two of you, sitting there, and I can see you both want me. And I want you as well, both of you."

Diego's balls tightened on the confession, and while the inclusion of Ronan in the statement should have deflated his interest, it didn't. His desire for this woman was too strong.

"You don't have to choose," Ronan interjected, a note of pleading in his tone. Apparently, he was smarter than Diego or had a large enough supply of blood so that his brain worked simultaneously with his cock. He'd jumped ahead in Cassidy's speech.

"Wait, what are you trying to say…Cassidy?" Putting his glass on the coffee table between them, Diego leaned closer to see her eyes more clearly. He saw pain there, and his heart lurched.

"I'm saying I don't know how to make this work. The two of you have spent the day vying for my attention. You're sitting there quivering like dogs waiting for a treat. It's not fair to either of you."

Ronan put his drink down and shot to his feet.

"Damn it, Nieves, this is your fault."

Diego stood as well and faced off with Ronan. "Bullshit! Just because you asked her out? There's no calling dibs on women, Callaghan, you said it yourself. This is the twenty-first century. If Cassidy hadn't wanted to go out with me, she would have turned me down. It's just a game to you, anyway. You don't care for her, not really. It's only a competition for you. Winning is what matters."

Ronan's eyes blazed with fury. He took a step closer to Diego. "Fuck you! You don't get to say how I feel or what my motives are. Cassidy isn't some notch for my bedpost, and I don't want her just to screw with you, either, you egocentric asshole."

"Stop! Please don't fight. It makes everything worse."

Diego and Ronan broke away from each to stare at Cassidy. She was on her feet as well, and oh, Holy Mother of God, there were tears in her eyes. An icy ball formed in the pit of his stomach. He'd done that to her. Ronan was guilty, too, but Diego only cared about his own role in causing her misery.

"Don't cry," he practically begged.

"Please, don't," Ronan chimed in. Diego heard the pain in the other man's voice.

Cassidy swiped at her cheeks with impatient strokes. "I'm sorry. I cry easily, and this situation is hurting me too much. I don't like setting you two against each other."

"You aren't," Diego rushed to assure her.

"This is all on us," Ronan added.

Cassidy shook her head almost violently. "No, it's not. This is my fault. I guess I kind of went a little crazy after being engaged for so long. But I'm not cut out for stringing two guys along, and there is no way I can choose between you. If I had a clear preference over you, then yes, I could cut the other loose with a lot of regret for taking it so far."

She lifted her face to them and sincerity as well as misery shone through. "I'm like the donkey standing between two stacks of hay. If I don't do something now, it will end badly for all of us. As hard as this is, as painful as this is, I know it's the right thing to do."

In a fit of near panic, Diego started babbling about why she didn't need to break up with both of them. He made incoherent promises that he knew he likely couldn't keep. Although it was all white noise to him. Ronan was doing the same. Like supplicants, they had their hands out to her, begging her to reconsider. She kept shaking her head, the tears falling down her cheeks.

"Please, just stop!" She practically screamed her plea. It shut both men up. "I need you to go now. I'll lock up after you're gone," she said in a quieter voice.

Diego hesitated as did Ronan, both staring back at her and hoping, what? That somehow she'd change her mind even knowing she wouldn't. Finally, Diego moved to leave. He hesitated a fraction of a second to make sure Ronan was doing the same. When it was clear the other man was following him, Diego trudged out of the room and down the stairs. He was weighed down with misery, and his foolish mind still worked for a solution that didn't involve giving up Cassidy. There was nothing, of course. She called the shots, and he felt guilty for his role in making her miserable.

When they reached the foyer, Diego stopped,

wondering how he was going to get home. For sure, he had no intention of getting into a car with Ronan, even if the fucker wanted to give him a ride, which he undoubtedly didn't. Ronan must have had a similar notion because, grabbing Diego's arm, he whirled him against the wall. Caught by surprise, Diego couldn't stop it.

"What the fuck!" he hissed between clenched teeth. He didn't want Cassidy to hear this.

Ronan got into his face. "You're going to have to find your own way home, asshole. I don't trust myself in your company right now."

Standing up straight, Diego clenched his fists. The urge to clean Ronan's clock was almost overwhelming. The way Ronan flexed his neck, he obviously had the same impulses. The last thing the shitty evening needed was to bloody Cassidy's beautiful marble floor.

"Fine by me." He started for the front door. "I'll put in a request to change partners as soon as I get in tomorrow."

"Feel free, but I may beat you to it."

And, with that final taunt, they split company. As soon as he left Cassidy's home, Diego started to shake. Part of it was unspent adrenaline. The other part was something he thought he'd put behind him. Unbearable sadness and regret and a keening need to turn back time and make different choices. Except unlike with the shooting back in New York, he couldn't muster regret for his actions. Pursuing Cassidy may have been a bad idea. It certainly hadn't ended well. Being with her, though, had been special. He would carry those memories as happy ones. Knowing that difference existed helped him to calm down and ease his body into a steady state.

Besides, he needed to get his shit together if he was going to manage to get a new partner without his lieutenant marking him down as a complete loser. He would be blamed for the partnership with Ronan not working, of course, he would. He was the new guy, the outsider, while Ronan was a Callaghan.

Shit, and they hadn't even found O'Malley's killer. A busted partnership coupled with an unsolved case was not the way to restart a career. Just one more reason to be mad at himself.

Chapter Six

Ronan kept the smile on his aching face as he walked into the station. He'd learned to hide his feelings throughout the long years after his parents' death. He'd hated the looks of pity thrown his way, and Daire frankly had dour down enough for all the brothers, so Ronan cultivated the carefree whenever he could. The ability served him well this morning.

He'd slept hardly at all, tossing around in his bed, seeing the heartbreaking sadness on Cassidy's face as she'd reluctantly, yet firmly cut him and Diego off at the knees. Or the balls maybe. His cock had shriveled up at the sight of those damn tears, that's for sure. Seeing a woman cry, knowing he'd made her cry, was worse than facing down a perp with a gun.

He took a long pull of iced coffee. This morning was going to suck way too much for even caffeine to fix. He had to face Diego and their lieutenant, because he wasn't going to be able to continue working with the guy. God, it was like being back in high school, moving seats in class to get away from someone who'd pissed you off. He felt stupid, and in hindsight, the whole fiasco was perfectly predictable.

The problem was that the only way to have avoided it was to have given up seeing Cassidy at all after Diego, the dick, had horned in. It would have been the sensible course of action, except when he'd told Diego last night that Cassidy wasn't merely a conquest, he'd meant it. Right from the start he felt something for her that was different, more than other women.

Now, he'd lost her and the man who was at least fifty percent responsible for it was sitting at his desk, brooding over his own cup of coffee. Ronan put a sneer on his face. Before he could think of a suitable opening line, his phone pinged. Pulling it out, he saw the text. He blinked a few times to make sure he was reading the message right. A string of swears flew out of his mouth as he sped up to Diego.

"We need to get to forensics," he barked out.

His still-partner looked up at him in surprise. A second later, he was on his feet, following Ronan. "What's up?"

"Frankie just texted me." Ronan headed for the elevator without missing a step "There's trouble with O'Malley's laptop—netbook—whatever the fuck it is."

He didn't say more because he didn't know any more. They went in silence, although Ronan had put aside any grief over Cassidy in the face of the investigation and figured Diego had done the same. They were professionals, and the job came first. They raced over to Frankie's station the moment they arrived.

The tech guy looked up at them and blinked behind his glasses. "That was fast."

"What's the problem?" Ronan barked out. The computer they'd recovered from O'Malley's apartment was open, the screen blank.

Frankie gestured toward it. "The thing's fried."

"What do you mean?" demanded Diego. "You've been digging into the files all week."

Frankie pushed the bridge of his glasses with his

forefinger. "Yeah, I was. Now, I can't 'cause it's fried."

"How did that happen, exactly?" Ronan asked, his patience dwindling.

"That's a good question. I don't know."

"Frankie!" Ronan put some mean in his voice. These tech guys could be maddeningly sanguine about stuff.

"I'm telling you, I don't know. I left for the weekend, and it was fine. This morning, it's fried." He shrugged.

A torrent of Spanish rushed out of Diego's mouth, no doubt the same words Ronan had said when he'd received the text. "Somebody came in over the weekend and did this deliberately, didn't they?"

"I can't say for certain that it was deliberate, but I can say it was thorough. I might be able to retrieve bits of data off it, but it will take a lot of time."

Ronan turned to Diego. "Son-of-a-bitch, looks like Mahurin not only took the bait, he took it a little too well."

"Yeah, but I don't see him doing this. He didn't strike me as the type to know computers well enough, and it would be strange for him to come to this station on a Sunday night, or any night really. There must be other cops involved," Diego added quite unnecessarily.

Ronan had already done the math. "When Finn went undercover, it was because Michael said there was a leak in the department. The fucker nearly got Finn killed."

"You think it's the same person?" Diego seemed skeptical.

"Who the hell knows? There's at least one dirty cop around here, that much is certain." He turned his attention back to Frankie. "Can you get started right away on trying to recover files?"

"I don't have to." Before Ronan could bare his teeth, the technician pulled a black plastic box out of his desk drawer. "I backed up all the files on this hard drive."

Ronan was speechless for a second. Then he broke out into a wide grin. "Frankie, you are the first man I've ever considered kissing full on the mouth."

Frankie blinked rapidly a few times. "Um, thanks, but I think you know what I'd prefer instead."

"Any ticket to any fucking thing in the world is yours."

Frankie beamed up at him. "You know what I want."

Yeah, Ronan did know. "Lady Gaga it is."

With a slap on Frankie's back that nearly sent the man sprawling, Ronan turned once more to Diego. His partner was smiling, too, relieved as Ronan was that the data hadn't been lost and hopeful once more that there was something worth seeing on the computer after all. If someone dared to tamper with evidence, they were running scared. Now was not the time to ask for a partner reassignment.

"Let's leave Frankie to it," he suggested.

"Right." The one word confirmed Diego was on the same page about putting aside their personal problems for a while.

"Smart of them to just screw with it instead of taking it outright," Diego said as they left Frankie.

"Yeah, there is no way to prove the frying took place here or was part of a virus that was already in the computer when we found it. And, with all the people coming and going here and in the evidence locker, there's no end of suspects."

"I hate the idea of a dirty cop."

"Me and you both," Ronan replied and, of course, it reminded him of his parents. He stopped suddenly and grabbed Diego's arm. "If Mahurin is behind this cover-up for O'Malley's murder, it may mean he had something to do with my parents' murders as well."

Diego glanced down at where Ronan held him, and for a second, they were both thinking of the last time Ronan put his hands him. Ronan released him in an instant.

Diego took a half-step away. "You think dear Uncle Connor was involved in that? Weren't they friends?"

Ronan shrugged. "I thought they were. Dad thought they were." He flashed on his father's heartsick statements to his mother about rotten cops. Could it have been more personal than blue pride?

"Let's hope Frankie finds something," Diego said in a soft voice that conveyed his sympathy, which made Ronan cringe even as he appreciated it. Diego didn't dwell on it, however, and Ronan appreciated that even more. "Lady Gaga?"

With a wry smile, Ronan shrugged again. Shit, if not for the feud over Cassidy, he and Diego would make great partners. He wanted to put the personal stuff aside. He couldn't. If Cassidy had been what Diego said—a notch on his belt—then okay, he could've put it behind them. She wasn't that, however, and there was no changing the truth.

They were quiet on the way back to their desks, and Ronan tried to keep himself busy by catching up on loathsome paperwork. He was mindful of Diego's presence, yet not as resentful as he had been. The job came first, at least for now it did. He felt more than saw or heard his partner rolling his chair closer to Ronan's. He glanced up. "What's up?"

Diego wore an earnest and uncomfortable expression, as if he had a difficult task ahead. Crap. If the guy started in on a conversation about Cassidy, Ronan didn't think he could keep his shit together.

Diego cleared his throat. Not a good sign. "I, ah, need to talk to you, but I don't want to upset you because I could be way off base about this."

Christ, Jesus, not now. There was too much going on for a heart-to-heart or fist-to-fist over Cassidy.

"It's about your parents."

Ronan blinked at his partner a few times in surprise. So, not what he thought.

"I've been doing some math, and it's not adding up. Assuming that O'Malley dropped off the grid around the time of the murders because he was somehow involved. Which is a big assumption, but my gut's telling me it's a good one. Then he was paid off for something by Mahurin or somebody else. Maybe he set your parents up or…" He licked his lips and took his gaze off Ronan for a second. "Maybe he even pulled the trigger."

Ronan's gut tightened, and the pain rolled through him as it always did when he thought of how his parents had died. Daire had been the one to identify the bodies and had kept the details from his younger brothers. Of course, Ronan had looked up the incident report the moment he had access to the file as a cop. Multiple bullet wounds, front-facing so they'd seen it coming. His mother, God, his beautiful mother, had scrapes along her face, arm, and leg where her body had landed on the pavement.

He closed his eyes a moment to pull himself together. Diego didn't say anything more, nor did he try to lay a hand on Ronan in comfort. Ronan appreciated the restraint. It almost made him want to forgive the man for Cassidy. Almost.

He opened his eyes and saw Diego staring back at him, patiently waiting. "Those thoughts have crossed my mind, too. O'Malley was a small timer, though, no violent crimes in his record. As disgusting a thought as it is, Mahurin would have been better suited to murder than O'Malley."

Diego nodded. "Maybe he just provided information."

Ronan tapped his finger on the arm of his chair. "On the other hand, with the right incentive a man can do anything and using him would have been a smart move. My father would never have expected him to be a trigger man."

"I thought that, too. The thing is even a double murder doesn't pay out what O'Malley has been spending for the last eight years." Diego leaned back in his chair. "Like I said, I've been doing the math, and rent, food, cable, porn, and the occasional call girl adds up to a lot even when done modestly. This isn't exactly *Day of the Jackal* stuff. Even a professional hit man isn't going to score big enough on one job to retire."

"You think he was taking other jobs all these years and not getting caught?"

"I was thinking more along the lines of blackmail."

"Huh." Ronan thought about it a minute. "How

could he get away with it? I don't think he was very bright and hanging out in Boston and blackmailing Mahurin or whoever pulled his strings to begin with? That's crazy. They would have tracked him down."

"They did track him down. It just took a long time. Remember Colleen being hassled by cops over the years, looking for him, even though he'd been laying low? Hiding in plain sight is a cliché for a reason, and it might have taken a few years before he started needing more money, right about the time he sent his sister that letter, I'll wager. He paid cash for everything as near as I can tell—no bank accounts, no credit cards. He got delivery a lot from the looks of his garbage and ordered his entertainment in, too."

"All right, I can see it, I suppose. But once they found him, why not make his body disappear? Why go to the trouble of making it seem like he was a vagrant?"

Diego made a sound of frustration. "That's the part that doesn't make any sense. Unless."

"Unless?"

"His death is a warning to others."

"What others?" Even as he asked the question, he answered it in his mind. "My father was looking into something, something involving police corruption. Bad cops, plural. I overheard him talking to my mother a few months before they were killed." His voice caught on the last word, and he had to swallow a few times to continue. "Anyway, it sounded like there was a network of bad cops he knew and had respected, like Mahurin, I guess. It really bothered him because he cared so much about the integrity of the badge, you know?"

"Yeah, I get it. It makes my blood boil, too."

Before either of them could say anything more,

Ronan got a text. Pulling out his phone, he saw it was Frankie.

Got something!

Ronan jumped up. "Frankie."

He didn't need to say more. Diego tore after him as Ronan raced to the lab. Frankie was sitting with a shit-eating grin on his face when they arrived.

"I knew all that porn watching would pay off in the end."

He swiveled around to his desk top computer where he'd attached the external hard drive with the O'Malley files. He pressed a key and sat back to watch. Ronan and Diego crowded around him.

At first it was a typical porno scene with lots of hard, sweaty flesh and lackluster moaning. Then it switched suddenly to grainy black and white footage. Ronan and Diego both leaned in closer to make sense of the poor quality film. The scene was some alleyway between row houses that could have been Boston. It was hard to tell. A man came round the corner of one house and leaned against the outside. A few seconds ticked by before another man approached. There was a brief verbal exchange that couldn't be heard above the ambient noise of the street. Something passed between them, although what was impossible to tell. It looked like a small package. The man receiving whatever it was turned enough as he left for his face to be visible for a few seconds.

"Freeze it!" Ronan barked a second before Diego said the same.

The two of them leaned over Frankie even more so that their faces were inches from the screen. Ronan's stomach lurched at the sight, but he wasn't really surprised. Standing back, he gave his partner a grim look. "Mahurin, the fucking asshole."

"Looks to me he was taking a bribe or something."

"Or something. That confirms our suspicions, or at least it does for me. Mahurin was one of the dirty cops my father was referring to. I can't believe O'Malley was clever enough to get this footage and embed it into one of his downloads."

Frankie swung around to face them and pushed at his glasses with his finger. "He probably had some neighborhood kid do it. Any high schooler taking comp sci could manage it."

"It doesn't matter. It's there, and whoever fried the netbook was right to worry there was something incriminating." He glanced at Diego. "Strengthens your idea about blackmail."

"There may be more, too. Is that the end of the files?" Diego asked Frankie.

"No, there's more."

"Please, keep looking," Ronan said. "There may be other footage embedded."

Frankie made a face. "Whatever you say, but this is kind of putting me off porn, like smoking too many cigarettes at once."

Ronan slapped the tech on the shoulder. "Sorry, pal. And thanks. This is huge. Keep it to yourself, though. I don't want anyone to realize what we've found until we confront this guy."

"Sure, whatever." Frankie turned back and hit play. Porno music started up again.

Ronan shot Diego an evil grin. "Let's go talk to dear Uncle Connor."

****

Diego held on for dear life, his default position when riding with his partner. He'd almost offered to drive, then thought better of it. Ronan was a good cop, and Diego didn't want to imply otherwise. Even though this thing with O'Malley and Mahurin were pushing a lot of hot emotional buttons for Ronan, he could handle it. If Diego had really thought he couldn't, he'd have said something back at the station. As opposed to discussing Cassidy, which was something they should do as two mature adults but probably wouldn't.

It sucked that she'd tossed them both, although it confirmed his view of her as being a nice person as well as a tempting woman. The idea of losing her ate at him. It shouldn't matter as much as it did given how little time they'd spent with each other. A couple of dates, three if you counted the birthday party. That wasn't exactly a forever scenario, and yet that was how it felt, as if he'd lost someone really important and special in his life. The damn thing of it was, he saw the same feeling in Ronan's eyes. It had been a low blow to accuse the man of only looking for a conquest. Although he'd meant it when he said it, he realized he'd been wrong. Ronan was hurting over Cassidy, too.

Diego had gone into work with the intent of asking the lieutenant for a new partner, even knowing it would look bad. He was already fighting the perception that he couldn't hack it as a cop because of the effect the shooting had on him. Asking for a change after one week would make him look like a basket case. And yet, the idea of working with Ronan had curdled in his stomach. Funny how the issue with the netbook and now the chance of making real progress had shoved everything else in the background. He wanted to solve this murder and the old Callaghan ones so much he could taste it. There'd be time later to fret over the Cassidy problem.

Ronan turned off the expressway with enough speed to make the wheels screech. Diego tightened his hold on the "oh shit" handle. They headed into a part of Boston that quickly took on more of a suburban feel. He was glad Ronan knew his way around the city. His network of contacts within the force was impressive as well.

It hadn't taken more than a single discreet phone call to learn Mahurin had called in sick for what was supposed to be his first day back from vacation. It was easy to look up the guy's address, and with luck, he'd be there. Neither Diego nor Ronan believed he was really sick so much as laying low because of the computer corruption, although what he hoped to achieve by hiding out remained to be seen. A smarter move would have been to act normally, not that Diego believed at this point he was dealing with smart people. Missing the computer had been stupid, and frying it proved to be a day late and a dollar short.

"His house is in the next block," Ronan said, slowing down the car. He took the corner at a quieter and more sedate pace, then cursed.

Diego followed his partner's gaze and saw Mahurin getting into a car. "God damn it, he was tipped off!"

"Not by Frankie, I'd swear to that. There are too many rats apparently running around to keep anything quiet."

Ronan sped up once more and tried to block Mahurin in. Too late. The other car pealed out from the curb and roared down the narrow street.

"Fuck, he spotted us." Ronan practically stood up as he jammed the gas pedal down hard. His car flew forward, closing the gap with the other car.

Mahurin wasn't going to go quietly and obviously knew they were after him. There was no other explanation for the high speed chase he was leading them on. The cars barreled through the neighborhood. Diego grabbed the magnetic beacon and pressed it onto the roof of the car while Ronan hit the siren, although announcing themselves made no impression on Mahurin. No surprise there, but it did hopefully warn others away. At this speed, pedestrians and vehicles were at risk.

Ronan deftly maneuvered around all obstacles. Their quarry didn't seem to have the same qualms about causing danger to others. Diego winced as the other car came within a hair's breadth of a parked car. Then his heart lurched into his throat when a couple started to enter a cross walk just as Mahurin raced by. They leaped out of the way with a second to spare and a startled yell.

"He's heading to the expressway," Ronan said, slapping the steering wheel. "If he gets on we'll have a harder time catching him."

Diego spared Ronan a glance. "You have a plan to stop that?"

"Yeah, catch up with him." By some unseen magic, Ronan pulled more horse power out of his car and managed to get close enough to Mahurin's that he tapped the bumper.

Diego grunted at the impact but otherwise said nothing. He understood that a greater need drove Ronan to catch Mahurin than Diego's. And he admired his partner's superior driving skills. He knew his vehicle and was keeping it under control. The same could not be said for Mahurin. The older cop took a corner too fast and, with the same kind of slow motion horror Diego remembered from the night of the shooting, the inevitable bad thing played out.

The car flipped and rolled, crashing into another car parked on the side of the street. The sound of screeching metal made Diego wince. There was a chain reaction of cars being shoved this way and that. Mahurin's kept rolling in the ensuing melee until it was right side up. Its journey ended when it skidded against a street light. Ronan deftly brought his car to a stop a few feet away from the first wreck and jumped out. Diego was right behind him.

With his gun at the ready, Ronan ran to the driver's side of Mahurin's car. He peered into the window, then holstering his gun again, wrenched open the dented door. Diego had his gun out as well and kept it trained on the car as he watched his partner struggle to get the door fully open. Mahurin lay against the back of his seat, blood streaming down his face. The damn idiot hadn't been wearing his seatbelt from what Diego could see. As Ronan crouched down to talk to the older cop, Diego called in for an ambulance.

There was a roar of fury, and Ronan leaned into the car, his hands fisting the other man's shirt.

Diego holstered his gun and quickly loomed over his partner. "Ronan, what the fuck?"

"Don't you dare die on me, you miserable fucker!" Ronan yelled, his face inches from Mahurin's. Ronan shook the guy. "Do you hear me? You can't tell me that and die."

Reaching down, Diego took hold of Ronan's arms. "Jesus, Ronan, stop. If he's not dead already, you're going to kill him."

Diego yanked on Ronan to pull him back. With his grip still tight on Mahurin's shirt, any movement of Ronan brought the dirty cop with him. Diego changed tactic and moved over to clasp one of Ronan's hands instead. He had to pry the fingers loose using both of his hands. As soon as he did, he wedged his body between Ronan and the car to keep him from grabbing on again as Diego worked on the other hand. Sirens wailed in the distance. Thank God backup was on its way, but he couldn't let anyone else see his struggle with Ronan. Bad enough that a crowd of gawkers had convened.

Ronan was like a madman, thrashing against Diego, desperate to get to Mahurin again. Diego was pretty sure the older man was dead, but there was no reasoning with his partner. So he didn't even try. He just used his superior strength to push Ronan away from the car. It was like being back in high school football practice and shoving the tackling dummy. He barely managed to get Ronan back to their car just as the first cruiser and the EMTs arrived. The uniforms did their job without being told, cordoning off the spectators and giving the EMTs a clear path. Knowing everything else was under control, Diego concentrated on his partner.

"Ronan, stop," he ordered as he pressed the other man against the car on the passenger's side. It was the farthest from the scene. He didn't want to be overheard and hoped none of the other cops would notice the weirdness playing out. Ronan's chest rose and fell on harsh breaths, and his whole body trembled. Slowly, though, he stopped fighting Diego. And just like that, he seemed to deflate. Diego opened the door to the back seat and nudged Ronan to sit down sideways.

Leaning on the door, Diego watched the EMTs place Mahurin in a body bag. When a uniform headed in their direction, he shook his head to wave him away. Then he grabbed the strobe light off the car. Everyone knew they were cops at this point, and the damn thing was giving him a headache. He studiously ignored the fact that Ronan had tears running down his face and gave him a few minutes to pull himself together before demanding an explanation.

"What the hell happened back there?" he finally asked.

Ronan scrubbed his face with his hands and sniffed back his tears. His voice hitched at his first attempt to speak. He cleared his throat. "He said he should have killed O'Malley years ago. Then he told me that my father was a good cop, clean, the best cop he'd ever known, and that was what got him killed."

Diego took a second to digest the information. When Ronan said nothing more, he asked, "Was that it? Did he say anything else?"

Ronan shook his head. "No, the fucker passed out or died or I don't know what."

"He's dead," Diego said as gently as he could.

"Shit!" Ronan looked up at him with red-rimmed eyes. "This is the closest we've come in eight years to finding out what happened, and the asshole dies. God damn, son of a fucking bitch!"

Diego couldn't blame his partner for his anger and

frustration. It was maddening to Diego, and he didn't have nearly as much emotion invested in solving the old case. "I'm sorry," was all he could think to say, pathetic as those words were.

"Yeah, me, too." Ronan was quiet for a moment, staring at the pavement. "It's like this wound, you know? It never heals. You can go long stretches where you don't notice it, forget it's there, then the pain catches your breath when you don't expect it. I just want it over, so they can rest in peace and my brothers and I can move past it."

He shifted in the seat, arms resting on his thighs. "I can remember Daire coming home. Finn and I were watching television while our parents were out having date night. We thought it was funny and cute that, after all those years of marriage, they still went out on dates.

"The door opened, and instead of Mom and Dad coming home, it was Daire. I knew something was wrong right away. It wasn't just the look on his face. I knew he should still be on his shift. He was new to the badge and gung-ho, no way he'd sneak in a break at home. Finn hadn't noticed. He was laughing at the sitcom we were watching, and there's Daire with his grim face walking slowly toward us. I thought it was an accident, that they were hurt maybe. He switched off the TV and said they were dead."

Ronan sniffed and swiped at his nose with his sleeve. "There was this buzzing in my head, like white noise, drowning out his words. Then I heard the word shot, and the noise cleared. Everything came into sharp focus, and all I wanted was revenge, not justice, revenge." He shook his head and huffed. "All those generations of cops, and all I wanted was to kill the motherfucker responsible with my bare hands."

Looking up at Diego, he shrugged. "It was a fine funeral, the best Boston could do for a fallen cop and his wife. The fucking rumors started that very afternoon, although I didn't know it at the time. As the weeks went by, then months and now years, no one caught, no answers, my brothers and I became more determined to figure it out on our own. And in all that time, this is as close to an answer as any of us have gotten."

He pounded his fist on the side of the door. "Fuck Mahurin for dying with nothing more than confirmation of what I already knew. My father wasn't dirty."

Crouching down in front of his partner, Diego said, "No, he wasn't. I think it's likely that Mahurin killed O'Malley or had him killed, but he didn't act alone." He sighed and rubbed his hand down his face. "So, we tackle Mahurin's home, his bank accounts, everything we can find. Maybe in the end, he'll tell us more than he intended."

Ronan gave him a grim smile. "Yeah, maybe." He stared at the ground for a while. "Ah, look, thanks for handling me. I lost it."

"You had good reason." When Ronan only rolled his eyes, Diego decided it was time to bare his soul, too. He knew something of what Ronan felt at the moment. "I moved to Boston because I couldn't stand staying in New York any longer. It reminded me too much about how I killed a kid."

Ronan's eyebrows went up, but he didn't say anything.

"He was fourteen, and yeah, packing a gun he'd used in a store robbery where his friend had killed a clerk. And yeah, he did something incredibly stupid by raising his gun instead of dropping it like I told him to. Still." The image of the boy crumpling to the ground rose unbidden in his mind. His gut clenched as it always did. He ignored his pain and pressed on because he thought it might help his partner.

"He was just a kid, with a baby face and a future cut short. Maybe he was going to die by someone else's hand that day. I wasn't the only cop cornering him, just the closest. I'm the one who shot him, though, and it haunted me. Haunts me. For months, I saw his face screwed up in agony every time I closed my eyes. The media coverage, the pain of his family, even the well-meaning support from fellow cops magnified the misery."

Ronan stared off in the distance. "You don't just see the pity in their eyes, you feel it too when your back is turned."

Diego nodded. "You enter a room and the voices stop. People look at you guiltily so you know they were talking about you."

"The same people who act supportive to your face feast on ugly gossip when you're not around."

"Right," Diego agreed with a huff. "I know what you mean about it being a thing that doesn't heal. Time and therapy has helped. Ultimately, I decided I needed a change in scenery. I hoped by leaving New York, I could break the obsessive patterns in my mind."

"Has it worked?"

"I think it has, yes. I wasn't sure I could handle being back in the field, but it's been fine. More than fine. I just wish this case had ended better."

"Me, too." Ronan grimaced. "Then there's

Cassidy."

Ah, shit. He'd almost forgotten about that little problem. "Yes, there's Cassidy."

"I think I'm falling in love with her." Ronan's confession was said so softly, Diego had trouble hearing it. It took a second for the words to sink in.

Diego sighed. "That's a problem, my friend, because I have, too."

Ronan threw his head back and barked out a laugh. "Oh, my God, we are so fucked."

Diego managed his own chuckle. "I guess we are."

"She's not going to change her mind about choosing between us," Ronan said, sobering up.

"No, she's not. And it's not fair to expect her to."

"Right, so there's really only one solution."

"We're going to fight for her?" Diego said it with a feral grin to show he didn't really mean it, except part of him did. He hadn't realized how powerful his primitive self was. He'd always prided himself on being civilized, especially when it came to women.

"Sure, that's a plan. We fight for her, the winner goes to her on bended knee, and when she finds out— and she will—that she was a prize that was won, she'll castrate both of us with the dullest scalpel she can find."

Diego winced at the statement, although he couldn't argue with it. "So what do we do?"

"This is going to sound crazy."

"Lay it on me. The day can't get much crazier than it is."

"We share her."

Diego fought to keep his expression neutral when he really wanted to roll his eyes at the not crazy idea, but stupid one, as if they could share a woman like they might share a car or custody of a kid or something. "Seriously? That's your solution? We pass her back and forth every other day and she rests on Sundays?"

Ronan didn't bother to hide his eye-roll. "Not like that." He leaned forward, excitement spreading across his face. "We share her all the time."

Diego thought maybe he was just too dense to get what Ronan was suggesting. "Because that worked so well yesterday."

"It was our competing for her that fucked up yesterday. I'm saying we share her on her terms. We park our testosterone and jealousy at the curb and let her call the shots. If she's the boss, we won't get into any fights."

"You make it seem so rational."

"It is if we buy into it. I'm not saying it will be easy. I'm saying she's worth doing it for."

For some idiotic reason, now that it was becoming clearer to him what Ronan was saying, Diego wasn't dismissing the idea entirely. It had disaster written all over it, and yet, if it was a way to have Cassidy, he had to at least think about it. Whether he had the discipline to make it work was another story altogether.

"How about sex? How's that supposed to work? Again, are you suggesting we share a rotating schedule in her bed?"

Ronan licked his lips and glanced away. "Um, tricky, but we do that together, too."

Diego snorted. "Really? A three-way?"

"Yes. I'm not suggesting we fuck each other, just her together."

The idea of getting naked and hard and performing

with another man in the room—touching the same woman—made Diego slightly queasy. He was all for gay rights, of course, but he was firmly heterosexual.

"Have you ever actually done that?"

"Sure." Ronan paused. "With two women."

"Of course. Why am I not surprised?" When Ronan shot him a cocky grin, Diego narrowed his eyes. "It's not the same, and you know it. Outside a porno, have you ever seen another guy fucking a woman with another guy in bed, let alone fucking her at the same time?"

"No, not as such. And I understand the point, I really do. We're talking about Cassidy, here. I'm desperate enough to try anything to keep her. If we don't buy into it fully, though, she's never going to agree to it."

Diego blew out a breath and became more aware of how many cops and firefighters and others had joined the party since he and Ronan had started their tête-a-tête. "Look, I'm not saying no. I need to think about it. In the meantime, we have work to do. Are you okay?"

Slapping his palms on his thighs, Ronan stood up. Diego straightened up with him.

"Yeah, let's put this motherfucking case to bed as best we can and tackle Cassidy with a clean slate." He slapped his hand on Diego's shoulder. "Thanks, man, I mean it."

"Anytime, partner." Diego meant it, too. Whatever happened with Cassidy, he knew he had a good partnership with Ronan and he was going to make it work.

Chapter Seven

Cassidy stared long and hard at the contents of her refrigerator, somehow expecting to find food inside she hadn't bought herself and actually felt like eating. No such luck. It had been a brutal week of work, so she hadn't had time to go shopping and buy stuff to indulge in an orgy of stress eating. Everything was disgustingly healthy, nothing heavy in both fat *and* sugar. She'd already checked the freezer and the cupboards, too.

Of course, she could get dressed again and go out to get something. She'd thrown on boxers and a T-shirt as soon as she'd gotten home. It seemed like more trouble than it was worth to change back. And not a good idea to use food to relieve her misery.

It was all her own fault. She wasn't going to blame Diego and Ronan, much as she wanted to. It wouldn't be fair. She was the one who agreed to go out with both of them. She was the one who jumped into bed with both of them as well. She'd wanted to do something wild and different with her life. When she put her mind to a task, she achieved it. That's how she got through medical school and residency. That's how she'd managed to call off her eternal engagement with Thomas. And ultimately, it was how she ended up falling for different men at the same time.

Perhaps she wasn't ever going to be suited for casual sex. It seemed ludicrous to become so emotionally entangled in such a short period of time. Yet, she had. It hadn't been only about the sex, amazing as it had been with both men. It would have been easy to walk away from sex. Her heart was breaking, though. She'd felt the loss of Ronan and Diego all week. There was no hope for it, however. She'd meant it when she said she couldn't choose between them. When she tried to picture her life with only one of them, it felt incomplete. There was a space left that neither of them could fill on his own.

With a grunt of disgust, she grabbed the butter, eggs, and shredded cheddar cheese. An omelet would have to do. As she placed the skillet on the burner, her doorbell rang. She scrunched up her nose in irritation and decided to ignore it. She was in no mood for company. The pealing continued. As tempted as she was to dig in her heels and not answer the door, politeness was ingrained in her, so she caved. Given that she wasn't exactly dressed for company, she hoped her caller would understand when she didn't invite them in.

As she hit the final set of steps, she could see two large figures through the mullioned window. Her step faltered when her mind filled in the details she couldn't discern. Ridiculous. It wasn't them. It couldn't be them. She stopped to flick on her security monitor. Holy crap, it was them!

Her heart fluttered wildly with anticipation, even as her brain told her to settle down. Whatever the boys had come to say, it didn't matter. The relationships were over. They had to be, or everyone's heart would eventually shatter. As she opened the door, though, she couldn't help wishing she wasn't going to be greeting them without make-up, her hair up in a messy ponytail, and in her ratty sleepwear. Oh, well, maybe the sight of her would send them running. Nah, they were men. Their standards were never very high where sex was involved.

With a deep breath, she opened the door and tried for a polite smile. "Gentlemen, this is an unexpected surprise." How clever, as if there were such a thing as an expected surprise. She was flustered already. Not a good sign.

Ronan and Diego stood on her front stoop, looking adorable and sexy, respectively, as usual. They were casually dressed—Ronan in T-shirt and jeans and Diego in a button-down and chinos. Diego carried a dozen sterling silver roses mixed with baby's breath. Ronan held what had to be a two pound box of imported chocolates. Each of them wore an identical expression of hope and pleading, reminding her of the way her cocker spaniel used to greet her when she came home from school.

On a heavy sigh, she turned and said, "Come in."

She stomped her way back up to the kitchen, aware of how the two men followed close behind her. She returned to her task of making dinner and cracked six eggs into a bowl. May as well make enough for all of them. Nobody said anything while she briskly whisked. Smart men. They'd read her mood right and were leaving it up to her to give them leave to speak their minds. Part of her was very curious as to what they had to say. The other part of her was terrified to hear it.

"You'll find a vase in the top cupboard over there." She jerked with her chin. "Please put those flowers in water." Diego moved quickly and silently to his directed task. Cassidy eyed Ronan, who stood almost at attention, the box of candy clutched to his chest. "I'll take one of those now if you please. Coconut cream if you have it."

She started in on heating the saucepan with the butter on the cooktop built into her island. The sound of crinkling paper told her the second order was being obeyed. As she got ready to measure out the egg mixture for the first omelet, a small chocolate drifted into her line of vision. Without looking at the delivery boy, she bent down and snatched the candy up with her teeth. Two masculine grunts punched into the room. She smiled inwardly in satisfaction.

Omelets were quick and easy when one knew how to make them. It only took a few minutes for all three to be done and plated. Only once she'd turned off the burner did she bother to look up at her guests. Their gazes were locked on her, again just like her dog, waiting for a signal. Tossing two of the plates farther down the island, she pointed to the high back seats on the other side.

"Sit," she ordered and they did.

Figuring this was a night for wine, she poured them all a glass of chilled pinot blanc. Then taking her own seat opposite them, she ate her meal, forcing herself to take her time and not wolf it down the way she wanted. Whatever was going on, she needed to give herself a chance to get on an emotionally even keel. Besides, it might not be fair of her, but she kind of wanted to make them wait. They bore at least equal responsibility for the mess they were all in. Fortunately, the guys were willing to play it her way. They didn't say a word, simply ate their food and drank their wine, although she could feel their occasional glance her way.

When the last morsel had been swallowed, Cassidy shoved her plate to one side and took a large gulp of her wine. "Talk," she said, looking at the two of them over the rim of her glass.

The men traded looks. As if they'd rehearsed it, and maybe they had, they said, "I'm sorry," in unison.

"I acted like an asshole last Sunday," Ronan added.

"Me, too," Diego chimed in.

Putting her glass down, she twirled the stem, thinking of what she wanted to say in response. She decided to go with her heart and not play any more games. "I'm sorry as well. The whole situation is all my fault."

"No!" Again they spoke as one.

"I was too cavalier with your feelings. And my own, frankly. I thought I was cut out for playing the field and casual sex. I'm not. If I were, then dumping you both wouldn't have made me miserable all week."

Her confession cheered the two men up considerably. They broke out in identical grins of satisfaction. Oh, perfect. She'd just fed into their male egos.

"We've been the same," Ronan admitted.

"I hope you haven't been at each other's throats." God, now she sounded like an egotistical maniac. As if she had the ability to inspire that kind of passion in one man, let alone two.

Pursing his lips, Diego said, "Not exactly, although the thought of planting my fist in Ronan's face might have crossed my mind once or twice." Ronan gave him a "bring it on" kind of glance, but said nothing. "We were busy solving that case."

"Oh, good to hear."

"Yeah, technically, although it didn't wind up the way we'd hoped," Ronan added, and pain flashed across his face. "We'll tell you about it later. Tonight, we have something more important to discuss with you."

Finally, here came the heartfelt apology that wouldn't make her feel any better. If it helped them, though, she'd listen calmly and compassionately. Then once they left, she'd have a really good cry. Damn, the tears were threatening to show up already.

"Go ahead," she urged, her voice shakier than she wanted.

Ronan looked as if he were girding his loins. Obviously, they'd decided he would be the spokesman. "The thing is, Cassidy, we both like you a lot."

Diego cleared his throat and shot him a look.

"We've pretty much fallen in love with you," Ronan amended.

Oh, my. Her heart thudded wildly, and her breath quickened. It wasn't possible. They'd known each other for basically a week. It wasn't possible for them to have such strong feelings for her. And, yet, even as she thought it, she realized it was crazy to question their sincerity when she had the same feelings for each of them.

"I—I don't know what to say." She swallowed more wine to give herself a second. "I believe I've fallen in love with you, too. Each of you, as crazy as that sounds. I know I've missed both of you terribly even though we barely know each other."

The men grinned at her again, clearly delighted with her confession.

"Don't look at me like that. It's an impossible situation."

"No, it's not," Ronan assured her. He leaned closer, his eyes gleaming. "The solution is simple. Take us both."

"We tried that."

"No, we tried your dating each of us separately. We want you to date us together." His expression turned bashful. "We want you to let us make love to you together."

Cassidy's mouth dropped open. She stared back at them speechless. It was the craziest idea she'd ever heard of, except hadn't Todd the Drink Server already put the idea into her head? Men were men the world over it seemed, gay or straight. She'd treated the suggestion at the bar as more of a joke, and yet she hadn't tossed the idea from her memory. Besides, how much difference was there really between fucking two men on alternating nights and fucking them at the same time?

She might have been two minds about the idea, but her body had no qualms. Excitement flushed through her, leaving her wet. Her breasts tingled with the memory of how each of these men had lavished them, as well as the rest of her body, with devoted attention.

"You can't be serious," she finally said.

"I was skeptical at first," Diego admitted. "I've had the benefit of a few days to mull it over, however, and I honestly believe it can work."

Jazzed from the discussion, Cassidy jumped up and paced away from her seat. She turned back to them with her arms folded over her erect nipples, giving herself a quick goose. "Less than a week ago, you were practically at each other's throats. What makes you think you can share me like that?"

"Because you'll be the boss," Ronan explained. "We cede control to you entirely. You lead, we follow, inside the bedroom and out. Diego and I won't worry about how much time and attention each of us gets from you. We'll trust you to be fair."

"Seriously? You think that will work?"

Diego stood up and Ronan followed suit.

"We're committed to giving it a try," Diego said. "We know it may not be easy, but you matter too much for us to just walk away."

It was madness, utterly foolhardy. Three-way sex and a three-way relationship? Who could juggle such a thing? Of course, she'd heard that polyamory was more common than people thought. People did make it work. The question was, could she? Could these two men in front of her do it? The speculation would drive her mad. There was only one way to know for sure. Tonight would be the test, and if it failed, she'd be no more miserable than she already was.

And if it succeeded?

She took a deep breath, not even trying to hide it from the guys. This was a huge step she and they were about to take, and she wanted to convey to them she wasn't taking it lightly. "Okay. We'll try it. For tonight only. If things go well, we try the weekend. After that?" She shrugged.

The first expression that crossed both men's faces was relief, as if they'd been dreading her answer. Their faces quickly morphed into each man's version of a smile. Diego's was warm and melted her heart. Ronan's was edgier, sexier, and it revved up her heartbeat. Their differences made the possibility of this three-way arrangement working more likely as together, they made her feel extra special.

She headed out of the kitchen at a slow pace without saying another word. The men didn't hesitate to follow her. Their compliance made her smile. She led them up to her bedroom, a place each of them was familiar with. When she entered, however, it held a new sense of excitement, of danger even. She turned to look at her lovers and, just thinking the word in the plural, sent a frisson of arousal down her spine. Ronan and Diego stood a foot inside the room, their respective gazes locked on her face, waiting for her to give them the signal to continue.

It was sweet and a little intimidating. She wasn't used to being the center of such intense attention, and she also wasn't used to being handed the lead in a relationship. She hadn't exactly been a doormat with Thomas, of course. Theirs had been this really civilized, almost bloodless partnership. The idea of calling the shots with two hot men worshipping her at her command was heady stuff. Understanding they were determined to let her make the first move, she made it.

There was no way to choose between them based on need or desire, so she went in alphabetical order based on last name. It was as rational a choice as any. She sauntered up to Ronan, keeping her gaze on him, and gave him a quick kiss. Turning to Diego, she did the same. It wasn't much, but it was a start, and she liked the experience so much, she did it again. This time she started with Diego and she lingered, letting her lips slide across each man's until they parted and let her in. By the time she was done, all three of them were breathless.

She stepped back to slow things down and rev them up. Without giving a command, she led by example by pulling her T-shirt off. Braless as she was, she knew a moment of self-consciousness as the guys' laser-like focus homed in on her breasts. The heat in their eyes as they looked, however, overrode her second of embarrassment. She hooked her thumbs into the waistband of her boxers and shimmied out of them. Then she stood fully naked in front of her men.

Her men. Yes, she could get used to that concept pretty damn quick.

"Your turn, boys," she practically purred in a voice she didn't recognize as she yanked the scrunchy out of her hair and shook her head. Just like that, she'd turned into some kind of movie vixen. The thought thrilled her.

When Ronan and Diego hesitated, she put sternness into her voice. "Don't keep me waiting."

Ronan had trouble with authority, he admitted it freely. In this case, however, he jumped to obey. It was beyond hot the way Cassidy stood like a naked goddess issuing orders in a low, sultry voice he'd never heard her use. His cock was already stiff and aching. He knew without looking that Diego was in a similar state. They both grabbed their shirts first and tore them off. It was easy for Ronan to do given he'd opted for the comfort of a T-shirt. Diego was right there with him, though, pulling open his button-down fast enough to send a couple of buttons flying, then yanking the shirt over his head.

Yeah, they were both primed.

Jeans, shoes, and socks were next, and of course,

underwear. And now he couldn't avoid seeing out of the corner of his eye the impressive rod his partner sported. As he and Diego had discussed, neither of them had been in the same room as another man's hard cock. But he stuck with the plan, which was to focus on what really mattered—Cassidy. She was beautiful and sexy as hell, with her curvy body enticing a man to go through hell just to touch it. Her plump breasts bounced on her every breath, and the nipples were hard points. His mouth watered in anticipation of sucking on each one as soon as Cassidy allowed it.

Standing there, waiting for her direction was killing him. His body vibrated with the need to claim her. The same impatience radiated off Diego. Shit, this was hard, but they'd agreed it was the only way this thing had a chance of succeeding. Cassidy's gaze bounced back and forth between then, her lips curled up in a slight smile. She was getting off on the power she had over them, and that was hot as hell. He'd never seen himself as the submissive type and still didn't, but there was something about the confidence of the woman that cranked his arousal.

"I think," she finally said when the room had filled with the tension of three people's need. "I'm going to let you guys off your leash. Show me what you want from me."

Ronan needed no further coaxing. He strode over to her and, wrapping one arm around her shoulder, pulled her into a kiss while he cupped one breast. He claimed her left side only, however, leaving the right one open for Diego. His partner wasted no time, either, reaching Cassidy a half a second behind Ronan. Diego clasped her waist and dropping to his knees, took her right nipple into his mouth. Cassidy cried out, the vibration ricocheting inside Ronan's mouth. Liking the sound and the feel, he pinched her left nipple with thumb and forefinger to make her do it again.

Her hand grabbed his ass, and she dug her nails into his flesh. He hissed at the bite of pain and rocked his dick against her side. Except he didn't just rub against her soft skin, he felt something rougher and harder against his rod. Diego's arm. His mind shorted for a second at the jarring realization, and he tilted his hips back. Cassidy stopped him by pressing him forward again with her hand. She was right, of course. There was going to be a lot of accidental touching between him and his partner. If Ronan couldn't handle that, the whole effort was doomed.

He let her guide him to a place where he once more rubbed against both people, and this time, he concentrated on the feel of Cassidy and not Diego. His partner moaned long and low. Ronan popped open his eyes long enough to look down. It was Cassidy's hand fisting Diego's hair that had pulled the sound from the man, likely nothing more than that. What did it matter anyway? He was kissing Cassidy and fondling her breast, and if this was all he accomplished, it would almost be enough.

Almost.

Breaking the kiss, he pressed his forehead against Cassidy's. "We need to move this party to the bed."

With heavy-lidded eyes, Cassidy nodded her assent. Diego apparently agreed, because he let go of his treat and stood up. He didn't let go of her, though, and neither did Ronan as they led her backwards to her bed. She couldn't see where she was going, but she obviously trusted them to get her safely to their destination. The bed was only a few feet away. When they arrived, Ronan arched a brow at Diego. The other man gave a quick nod of assent and let go of Cassidy long enough for Ronan to scoop her up and deposit her as gently as he could in the middle of the bed.

He followed her down so that he lay on his side facing her. Diego raced around to the other side of the bed and mimicked Ronan's position. The fit was tight as it was only a queen-sized bed. Ronan made a mental note that if this relationship worked out, they'd need to go king. That detail could wait. For now, things were right as he'd hoped. Cassidy was lying restlessly between her two lovers, and her face wore an expression of impatient arousal. Ronan wasted no more time and latched onto the nearest breast.

For long minutes, he concentrated on the task of helping to make Cassidy writhe and moan. While he sucked and laved the hard nub between his lips, Diego did the same with the other one. Cassidy's legs moved restlessly, her need obvious. Ronan released the hold his hand had on the breast in his mouth and skimmed his fingers down her belly. His fingers brushed up against another set when he reached her mons. Startled, he flashed open his eyes and looked at Diego. The other man was eyeing him, too. With their gazes still locked, they moved their hands in unison, sliding their forefingers through Cassidy's slick folds.

She cried out and bucked as they fought a battle for ground over her clit. Her body shuddered and her legs closed, trapping Ronan's and Diego's hands between them. Both men smiled around their mouthfuls of breast. Damn, Cassidy was a hot reactor. Making her come was a pleasure all in itself. Ronan knew if they kept up their assault, she'd come again. As tempting as it was, he was selfish enough to want to join more in the fun. His cock throbbed with the need for release, and his hips bucked into her body of their own volition. Nothing would do, but to come inside her.

He let go of the nipple and laid a trail of kisses and licks up her neck and to her mouth. He kissed her hard and fast before whispering into her ear loud enough for Diego to hear.

"Let us in, please?"

Her breathing still labored from her orgasm, Cassidy nodded. "Diego first."

A spurt of indignation erupted inside of Ronan before he squashed it. This was the deal. Cassidy got to choose, and what she chose would always be right. Besides, she'd kissed him first, and he'd been allowed the honor of placing her on the bed. It was only fair that Diego was allowed to fuck her first.

"Ronan?"

He looked up and grinned at his partner. No, his friend. The man had the same fierce desire shining through his eyes that Ronan felt himself. "What?"

"Condoms," Diego said with a jerk of his chin.

"Right." Rolling over, Ronan yanked open the drawer to the night stand and pulled out the box of condoms. He took one out and tossed it to Diego, then got one for himself. As hard as he was, he may as well put it on now.

Once he was covered, Diego shifted between Cassidy's legs. She watched him with eyes that were mere slits, and her lips slightly parted. Kneeling, Diego lifted her legs and bent them toward her torso. The man's cock lined up with her cunt, but before he entered her, Ronan distracted Cassidy by cupping her chin and turning her face to him. He pressed her lips with his tongue and speared her mouth just as Diego thrust his cock in to the hilt.

Ronan swallowed another cry from Cassidy. Her body rocked to the rhythm of Diego's thrusts, and Ronan adopted the same pace with his tongue. He swiped his hand down to clasp her right breast, circling the nipple with his thumb. Cassidy's moans increased, and her breath hitched every time Diego bucked his body against hers. With the hold each man had on her, there was little movement her body could achieve. She fought against the holds, trying with ever greater wildness to throw them off her.

She somehow managed to get her hand up and grab onto Ronan's cock. When she came the second time, she squeezed tight enough to make him yell. His voice was joined by hers, then a third one chimed in. Diego groaned above them and shuddered with his orgasm hard enough to shake them all. He stayed still for a minute with his body pressed flush against Cassidy's, then pulling out, flopped onto his side. Diego didn't just lie there, though. As soon as he was down, he pulled Cassidy onto her side to face him.

Ronan made a sound distressingly like a whimper when he was forced to release Cassidy. But his mood shifted quickly when he realized what his friend had done. While Diego proceeded to kiss Cassidy and lavish attention with his hand on a breast, Ronan shifted her top leg forward. Scooting down a bit, he lined his cock up with her glistening pussy. Her folds were swollen and wet from her orgasms, inviting him to come into the sweet warmth. He slid in on a sigh.

Her cunt was slick, yet tight. It welcomed him in with a greedy grasp of his aching dick. He wanted to pump fast and hard and come with the intensity he'd experienced with her before. Instead, he made himself go nice and easy with slow strokes in and out. His orgasm built gradually, giving him the promise of an intense ending. Once more, Cassidy moved restlessly between the two men, clearly not yet satiated. She was the perfect woman for two men, so quick to react and so slow to satiate.

Ronan cupped her ass and gave it a squeeze, then moved his hand to her front. As with before, he ran into Diego's hand. His friend opened his eyes as he continued to ravish Cassidy's mouth. He winked at Ronan and moved his hand to play with Cassidy's breast again, leaving her clit to Ronan. Everywhere that Ronan touched was plump and drenching wet. Her clit was nestled deep within the engorged tissue, but Ronan found it and clenched it between two fingers. He rubbed and squeezed while he picked up the tempo of his thrusts.

Suddenly, slow and easy became impossible to maintain. He needed fast and rough, and God bless her, Cassidy kept right up with him. When her pussy clenched down on his cock with her third orgasm, he lost what little control he had. He bucked against her soft ass as his release pulsed through him. He buried his cock deep within her, as if he could shoot his cum up to her womb.

With his head bowed back, his hips slammed once more against her. His chest was plastered against her back and still he tried to get closer to her. A hand, large with strong fingers, grabbed his waist and pulled him forward. Diego. His friend understood his need and was lending his help. It should have creeped him out to be touched by another man, but it didn't. With the hum of the orgasm still singing through Ronan's body, it felt just right.

****

In the end, it was easy, natural even, for the three of them to make love together. Diego could only shake his head at the amount of time he'd spent in the last few days worrying over this "crazy" idea Ronan had about how to keep Cassidy. All he'd had to do was let go of insecurities and possessiveness and let it all happen. It was Cassidy, of course, who'd made it work. She'd led them long enough and far enough for the men to take over and love her the way she deserved. They'd each showered her with as much attention as they could, proving their love and proving themselves worthy of hers.

After their first foray Friday night, they'd slept long and well, with Cassidy cradled between them. The bed wasn't quite big enough, so they'd squished in, which meant he and Ronan had occasionally touched just as they had while making love to Cassidy. At first, his natural reaction was to pull back as if burned. Then he'd gotten over that foolishness and understood that physical contact between him and Ronan was another way of cementing their respective bonds to the woman they loved.

The ties were tightened by all three of them by spending much of Saturday getting to know each other better and sharing important things that none of them had been able to really speak of before in their whirlwind romances. Ronan had told Cassidy about his parents' murder and how O'Malley's death might have tied into it. Diego had told her about the kid he'd killed in the line of duty and the way it haunted him still, although no bad dreams had disturbed him while he slept beside her.

For her part, Cassidy explained in more detail her somewhat stifling childhood, what had led her to be a medical examiner, and the scariness of letting her fiancé go after so many years. She was again apologetic about dating them both at the same time, something he and Ronan were quick to assure her she had nothing to apologize for. In fact, they were the ones who owed her an apology for competing over her, as if she were a prize, then fighting when the game became too intense for them.

Talking about their issues had cleared the air. There was nothing left except mutual affection and the scorching heat being generated by the three of them entwined once more in Cassidy's bed—their bed.

Diego sat propped up against the headboard with his legs splayed open and his knees bent. Cassidy's silky body was nestled up between them, her back to his front and with her head tucked under his chin. He held her tight against him by cupping her breasts in each hand. He teased both nipples with flicks of his thumbs. His cock was trapped between their bodies and every time she undulated against him, his arousal jacked up.

Diego rubbed his cheek against her hair and looked down at the black head bobbing between her legs. Ronan held Cassidy open and pressed against Diego. He feasted on her clit with enviable enthusiasm. Diego hadn't had an opportunity to taste for himself that day, but he felt no concern about the lack of opportunity. His time would come, maybe even before the night was over. In the meantime, he could enjoy the show and add to their lover's pleasure with his breast play.

Cassidy moaned and arched her back as much as their mutual hold on her would allow. Ronan had done something especially intense apparently. The man lifted his head enough to glance up at Diego. His eyes sparkled with mischief. Diego grinned back at him in the shared pleasure of driving their woman to distraction. Breaking eye contact, Ronan picked up speed, his head bobbing and weaving at an almost frantic pace. Cassidy writhed in sync with whatever the man did. She lifted her head and bowed forward with a scream.

Diego stayed with her, bending forward as well. The shudders racking her body stimulated his cock so much he had to fight to keep from coming. Not yet, he wanted to do it inside her. Ronan sat up, his face wet with Cassidy's juices. The man's cock was hard and ruddy with a head glistening with pre-cum. He pushed the hair back from a still quivering Cassidy and clasping her face with his hands, pulled her in for a long and lingering kiss.

Diego slid his hands down to her belly, making little swirls around her abdomen to soothe her past the orgasm. Cassidy whimpered and clenching her hands around his, she moved him farther down. Understanding that she wanted more, not less, he cupped her mons and squeezed her clit. She bucked back into him, urging him on. He could have caused her to come again, but his dick made him selfish. He let go with one hand to grab a condom off the nightstand.

Damn, he had to let go of her completely if he was going to get it open. Except Ronan reached over and took it from him. Together they managed to open it with one hand from each of them. The awkward yet effective effort made Diego chuckle. Ronan mimicked the sound as he continued to ravage Cassidy's mouth. She broke the kiss, however, just as Diego rolled the condom on.

"Scoot back," she ordered Ronan in a breathless voice that shot straight to Diego's cock.

Ronan hurried to comply. Cassidy broke free of Diego's embrace enough to shift her legs under her. Then she bent over, giving Diego a perfect view of not just her lovely ass, but her plump and wet cunt, as well. She placed her hands on Ronan's thighs and looked over her shoulder.

"Fuck me, Diego, while I reciprocate Ronan's efforts." With her hair messed up and her lips swollen, she was a vision of wantonness.

Diego didn't need any further urging. Drawing up his legs, he shifted to a kneeling position behind Cassidy. He placed his hands on her ass cheeks, and while his cock urged him to mount her hard and fast, he resisted. He wanted a moment to appreciate the beauty before him. With gentle strokes, he caressed the globes, admiring the softness of her skin. He skimmed his thumbs down the crease and dared to stop to tease the puckered hole. It quivered with his touch, and for the first time in his life, he wondered seriously what it would be like to sink his cock in this tighter place. The thought electrified him, but that was for another day.

"Christ!" Ronan exclaimed.

Sitting back on his heels, the man braced his arms against the footboard. His head was thrown back, and his chest rose and fell with harsh breaths. Diego couldn't blame him. With Cassidy's luscious lips wrapped around his dick, the guy's brain must be scrambled. Her head bobbed with the same enthusiasm as Ronan had shown moments earlier as he ate her out. Wet sucking sounds reverberated through the room. Diego's cock throbbed, reminding him that he was not yet in the game.

He lined it up with Cassidy's sweet pussy and pushed it all the way in with one long stroke. Cassidy moaned around her hard mouthful and shoved her ass back to seat him even farther inside. For a few seconds, he stayed still, enjoying the sensation of being cocooned within her slick warmth. She squeezed her cunt against his cock, making him grunt. When she did it again, he got the message and began a steady rhythm of thrusting.

His orgasm built slowly. He wanted to draw it out. Ronan and Cassidy made it impossible. Between his friend's mounting groans and her counter thrusts punctuated by squeezes of his cock, he couldn't hold out. So he picked up the pace, drilling into Cassidy with short, hard strokes. He clasped her hips with a firm grip to control their pace, pulling her toward him with every thrust forward.

Ronan shouted out as Cassidy swallowed him down deep. Knowing his friend was coming drove him to the edge, but he didn't want to come before Cassidy did. He seated himself to the hilt and slid one hand down to finger her clit. She dripped with her earlier release. He found the nub and rubbed small circles around it. As soon as he did, her body began to shake.

Ronan sat up and pulled Cassidy off his cock. He brought her face up to his and devoured her mouth. With her torso raised, Diego had even greater access to her front, so he added a second finger to her folds and stroked her clit. Seconds later, she cried out, the sound barely swallowed by Ronan's mouth. Her cunt clenched down on Diego's cock, and that was all it took to send his release spiraling out of him. He pumped with desperate and erratic strokes as he milked the orgasm from his balls and through his cock. A stream of Spanish imprecations flew out of his mouth. For a few seconds, he was lost in the sensations, barely aware of where he was and with whom.

Then he heard a masculine laugh, followed by a feminine one. Diego pried open the eyes he'd shut involuntarily. Ronan and Cassidy had their arms wrapped around each other's shoulders, with Cassidy's head tucked under Ronan's chin. They looked so beautiful together, so right.

Ronan grinned at him over Cassidy's shoulder. "I have no idea what you just said, but I'm assuming it was good for you?"

Diego grinned back. "It was, and if we're going to stay together, I'm going to have to teach both of you some Spanish."

"Hmm," Cassidy purred. "I took Spanish for a few years in school, but I don't think I ever learned those particular words."

Diego shifted his arms to wrap them around her waist and leaned in to kiss her shoulder right above where Ronan's arm rested. His throat rubbed against that arm, and yet the accidental touch didn't bother him, not anymore. He was too well-fucked. "Well, you're going to hear them a lot from now on. You make me lose control, *querida*."

Cassidy moved one hand to caress Diego's arm. "Good. I like that. I love that. And I love being with both of you."

Even said as it was in a low and sleepy voice, it had the power to make him ridiculously happy. He glanced up at Ronan and saw those same feelings in his eyes. Had it really only been a couple of short weeks since he'd worried that he wouldn't get the new start in Boston he craved? Things had worked out in a strange, yet wonderful way. This was right—the three of them could make a family.

"So do I," he said, looking straight at Ronan.

Slipping one arm from around Cassidy, Ronan clasped his hand on the back of Diego's neck. It wasn't a sexual gesture, but a fraternal one. Ronan didn't say anything, he didn't have to. His expression said it all.

It said "welcome."

Epilogue

Ronan was nervous. Weird. It was only a small family gathering. A backyard barbeque with his brothers and Regan, Uncle Jack, Caruso and Craig before the fall weather set in. Family. Just family. And that was why he was nervous, because he was bringing his new family.

Cassidy and Diego sat in the back of Ronan's car, each holding a pie. The driving configurations were still a tricky thing to work out. But all other things being equal, they'd manage to weave three lives in an effective and satisfying way. They were happy, deliriously so. It wasn't only the sex, either. They enjoyed each other's company. Diego had more in common with him than he'd realized, and if they could manage to survive baseball season, then life would be perfect.

He parked in the driveway of his childhood home and took a second to see it from the other's eyes. It was a neat and tidy home, a great place to grow up. Now he was gone from it for good. Slowly, he and Diego were moving their lives into Cassidy's beautiful townhouse. It only made sense, but a working class kid from Charlestown living in the Back Bay was, well, once again, weird.

By the time he got out of the car, Diego and Cassidy were on the sidewalk. They each held their pie in one hand and Diego's other hand rested on the small of her back. They smiled at him as he approached. They must have sensed his nerves. There wasn't anything he held back from them anymore and vice versa. If they were to be a family, they had to know and understand each other.

When he reached them, Cassidy slid her hand in his so that she was, as usual, sandwiched between her two men. "It's going to be fine, you know," she said with a squeeze of her hand. "They're your family, and they will accept you as you are."

"I know. They have to because you're my family, too, now."

Diego grunted. "I'm glad we're starting with yours, my man. Mine will be a harder sell."

"As will mine," Cassidy said on a sigh.

Ronan had no chance to respond. The front door opened before they got to it, and Regan stood in the doorway with eyebrows raised. "Hey, cuz. Cassidy. Diego." She greeted each of them in turn with a grin that became more wry as she went. "Oh, pie." She reached out to grab the desserts and went back into the house.

Ronan led the way inside. As much as he and Diego loved to keep their hands on Cassidy, it wasn't possible to go through the doorway three-abreast, so he let go. Ronan immediately took Cassidy's hand once more. They walked through the house and into the backyard. He stopped a moment to take in the scene.

Daire was manning the grill already, with Finn and Michael standing nearby, drinking beer and heckling him on his cooking skills. Regan had set the pies on the picnic table and was slapping Uncle Jack's hand as he tried to steal a piece of pie crust. Craig was off to the side of the yard playing tug of war with a medium-sized mutt. The kid looked happy, and Ronan remembered Finn saying something about getting him a dog.

It was all right and perfect except for one thing. He whistled once, sharp and loud. All talking stopped and even the dog turned to him.

"Sorry. I just have a little announcement to make." He glanced at a surprised Cassidy and Diego for a quick consent. They hadn't discussed making a statement about their relationship, but it suddenly felt right.

He cleared his throat. "Um, I just wanted to let you all know that Cassidy and Diego and I are moving in together and we've formed a family. The three of us," he clarified just in case his point hadn't been made. "We're a family now."

There was silence for a few seconds as everyone stared at them, frozen in place. Ronan's heartbeat sped up. Oh, shit, had he read his brothers and the others wrong? Would they be unwilling to accept the life he'd chosen?

Uncle Jack broke the quiet. "Well, Christ Jesus, boyo, you think we don't know that? We've got eyes, haven't we? Cassidy, darling, did you bake these pies?"

Cassidy blinked a few times. "Yes, I did."

"Then tell my daughter here that it's okay for me to have a slice before dinner."

Cassidy laughed. "Well, maybe just a sliver." She tugged her hands free and shot each of her men a sexy grin before heading over to the picnic table.

"Hey, Nieves, I could use another beer over here," Daire called out before turning back to his grilling.

"On it." Diego winked at Ronan before trotting

over to the cooler by the door.

Ronan stood where he was, watching everyone else. Cassidy laughing over something with Jack and Regan, Finn leaning into Michael, Daire taking the bottle from Diego before flipping a burger. Craig and the dog were on the ground wrestling over the hunk of rope. Something bumped his hip, someone. He turned to Diego and accepted the offered beer. They clinked the bottles together before taking a swig.

He knew a moment of perfect happiness until he remembered that life wasn't going to be perfect, nor completely happy. Not until they had the answers they needed. He'd been so close. But they knew more than they had before and someday they'd know it all.

For now, he was with his family, and it was enough.

Samantha Cayto

About the Author

I'm a corporate lawyer, happily married for over twenty years with three kids and four dogs. No white picket fence, but we do live in the burbs west of Boston. While my husband and I still do occasionally lick chocolate off each other, our more typical evening involves lying in bed once the kids are in theirs and reading separate books. Mine of course are romance. I started reading them as a defense against all those boring legal documents. Once I started, I couldn't stop.

I've also loved erotica since I was old enough to appreciate what sex is. I've been publishing erotic romance since 2009.

Besides my family, writing, and reading, my loves include the sight, smell, and sounds of the ocean (I'm a New England girl through and through), chocolate (naturally), prime rib (bloody), and good bourbon on the rocks.

Visit Samantha at
http://www.samanthacayto.com

To chat with Samantha Cayto and other Wild Rose Press authors of erotic romance, join us at www.groups.yahoo.com/group/thewilderroses.

Coming Soon

Cuffed & Collared
Book Three
Boston's Brave

by Samantha Cayto

Regan Malloy is a dedicated homicide detective married to her job. A tough woman who holds her own when it comes to the opposite sex, she is nevertheless resigned to lonely nights with fantasy men. When a serial killer targets wealthy submissive men from an upscale BDSM club, Regan is convinced the killer is a woman and goes undercover.

Kyle Ramsey is a topnotch litigator juggling life as a divorced father and a workaholic. Raised to be strong and to always take charge, he has trouble trusting that anyone else can get the job done. When he finds his good friend murdered, he mounts his own investigation despite Regan's warning not to interfere.

Regan is furious to find the sexy lawyer at the club but can't deny her attraction or her need to dominate him. Kyle discovers more than clues as, to keep from blowing their cover, the fiery cop demands obedience. Together they embark on a journey to explore this new world of hidden desires, but the road could take a dangerous turn when they cross paths with the killer.

Also Available

Blue Heat
Book One
Boston's Brave

by

Samantha Cayto

http://amzn.com/B00N2AH972

Finn Callaghan's quest to prove his father wasn't dirty and to follow family tradition leads him to become one of Boston's brave. Like his father and brothers, he proudly wears the blue but as an openly gay man. His first assignment—going undercover as a teenage runaway. The sexy detective in charge is a bonus and a distraction he just can't pass up.

Only half out of the closet, Michael Caruso heads a task force to end an underage prostitution ring that preys on homeless gay teens. He has mixed emotions about using the hot young rookie as bait. Finn is perfect for the part, but Michael's attraction to the pretty cop might botch months of work.

Attraction turns to alarm as Finn goes deeper undercover. Can Michael keep him safe? And even if he can, how can he protect himself from the danger falling in love?

Blue Heat

Prologue

There was nothing more perfect than a summer night in Boston, warm with a slight sea breeze to keep the sizzling heat at bay. Rory Callaghan loved walking the streets of his city, especially when he had his pretty wife on his arm. Sheila was still a beauty in her middle years, only slightly rounder than she had been in their youth. But then so was he and without the reason of having carried and birthed three children, their sons.

Jesus, God, just the thought of his fine boys, healthy and strong, made his chest swell with pride. It was a bit sexist, yes, to be proud as a peacock that he had fathered three carbon copies of himself. He was a bit old-fashioned, so there it was. No fighting it. And each one of those boys was destined to wear the badge as he did, as his father and his grandfather and just about every other Callaghan male had for more than a hundred years since coming over during the famine.

It was a fine tradition to carry on even if times were dicey. There was trouble afoot, a rot in the force that came from top to bottom and back up again. It needed to stop before it infected many more. He hadn't thought he'd be the one to take charge, but fate had her way of grabbing a guy by the short hairs and making him take notice. He'd deal with it. He had to. The shield meant too much to him to turn a blind eye and let it all slide.

Tonight, though, was for his lovely bride of

twenty-five years. He'd promised her a nice evening out, and he never went back on his word. Dinner had been expensive for a cop's salary, but she was more than worth it and had earned every morsel of pleasure he could give her.

Now, a nice turn around Columbus Park and the short drive back to their tidy house in Charlestown and maybe he'd get lucky. Luckier, of course. Any night he could lie beside the woman he loved, secure in knowing she was there and the boys were safely tucked in their own beds, was lucky enough for any man.

Squeezing her hand where it clasped his arm, he looked down at her and smiled. Still, a man could hope.

Except there was trouble looming in front of them. In a split second of time, everything changed. Hope turned to fear as the man approached. There was nothing to indicate danger other than the sense that twenty years of being a cop gave a man. He started to pull Sheila behind him even before the man showed his gun. Too slow. Damn it all, he was too late and too slow.

Sheila screamed when the first shot rang out. Rory pushed her down and flung himself at the man.

He didn't feel the first bullet or even the second, but his body seized and faltered and fell just the same. More shots and more screams. He twisted his neck to see his love and found her beautiful sightless eyes staring back at him.

No! God, no, it couldn't end this way. He'd failed to stop the rot and in that failure had thrown his woman into the danger. He'd trusted the wrong men or tipped his hand when he thought he'd been careful. Either way, it was over.

As he gazed up at his killer one last time, he thought of his boys. He would never see them wear the badge, wasn't sure they should if this was how it would end for them. God protect his brave boys.

Chapter One

Finn Callaghan jack-knifed up in bed, panting through the last of his nightmare. Beside his bed, his alarm screamed its way through his aching head. He slammed his palm on top of it without looking, a practiced move that silenced the damn thing.

Christ, he hadn't had the awful dream where he lived through his parents' murder through the eyes of his father in a long while. It didn't take a psych degree to understand why it had come back to plague him. Today was the day he followed the Callaghan tradition and pinned on the badge. Of course, he'd think of his father, the best cop he'd ever known. Rubbing the palms of his hands over his sweaty head, he tried to calm himself.

His bedroom door swung open after a perfunctory knock, and his brother, Daire, popped his head inside. "Oh, good, you're awake. Don't want to be late for your graduation."

"Seriously?" Finn rolled his eyes. "I've been getting myself up for years now. You don't have to mother hen me."

Daire leaned against the door jam and studied Finn with eyes that always saw too much, more than what Finn wanted them to see anyway. He was just like their father, which was why Daire was the second best cop Finn had ever known.

"Mothering is Ronan's job. Mine is to kick your ass when need be."

Yeah, he had a point there, except Ronan had moved out once Finn stopped needing the mothering. Or at least when Finn's brothers decided he didn't need it. By Finn's estimation that had been a good five years after he'd made the decision. But there was no telling his older brothers anything, not when their parents were dead and buried and Daire had assumed the post of head of the family.

"Well," he said, throwing the covers back. "I'm up, so my ass can remain bruise free." He slid off the bed and yawned loudly as he stretched. "No way am I going to be late for graduation, especially because I'm the one giving the valedictorian speech."

"And proud we are of that, boyo," Daire offered with a grin.

"Thanks, and you can lose the Irish lilt. Our family left the old country more than a hundred years ago."

Straightening, Daire shook his head and tsked. "You millennials have no respect for the old ways. Now get in the shower. I have breakfast waiting for you."

Finn perked up at the mention of food. Even at twenty-two, he still had a ravenous appetite. The grin he shot his brother was genuine. "I'll be down in ten."

He followed Daire out of his room, then peeled off in the opposite direction to the upstairs bathroom. The easy banter with his brother had helped the nightmare to dissipate. The shower would wash the rest of it away. Besides, there would be plenty of time to remember his parents and mourn their loss as the badge was pinned on his chest in a few hours. His brothers had tried to dissuade him from joining the force, but his path had never been in doubt.

He was a Callaghan, and Callaghans were cops.

****

Michael Caruso walked slowly down the hall that stank of piss and tobacco, his gun held at the ready. Shouts and curses echoed from the first floor as other cops in the raid contained the perps rounded up down there. He was sure they'd find someone up on the second floor, although he didn't know who or whether they'd prove to be dangerous, so he assumed the worst. His partner, Washington, breathed noisily behind him. The guy'd been nursing a head cold for the last few days and seriously sounded like Alfred Hitchcock.

Stopping beside the first closed door they found, he gestured to his partner with his head to move on to the next room. He pressed his ear closer to the door in case there was something to hear. When no sound came through, he grabbed the knob with his free hand and shoved the door open. He stepped into the room with his gun raised in both hands and scanned the area in a millisecond.

A terrified cry greeted him from the filthy bed shoved up against the far wall. It was the only piece of furniture in the small room. Michael spared its occupant a quick glance before he stepped farther into the room and took a closer look. There was nothing else there, not even a closet door. The space wasn't a real bedroom, except someone had turned it into one, although not for sleeping. Once he determined there was no danger, he dropped his gun to his side and approached the bed slowly.

A boy lay curled up on his side, naked and covered with bruises. He couldn't be older than fifteen or so, slender with light brown hair and wild eyes. He looked up at Michael and whimpered.

"Please don't hurt me," he begged in a rough and pleading voice. "I won't fight any more, I promise."

Slowing his steps, Michael held out his free hand in what he hoped was a soothing gesture. "It's okay. I'm not here to hurt you. I'm a cop. The whole place is filled with cops. You're safe. We're going to get you out."

Tears formed in the kids eyes. "You mean that?"

"Absolutely." Michal turned briefly to show the boy his back, where his jacket said Boston Police on it. "See?"

A sob tore out of the boy's mouth. "I can't go home. They don't want me there."

"It's okay. We'll find a safe place for you," Michael vowed and tried not to show how pissed he was, not just at the people who had taken advantage of this runaway, but also at the people who should have cared for the kid in the first place. He couldn't believe how parents could turn their kid out just because he was gay.

Washington popped his head in. "I've got four more boys down the hall." His gaze flicked briefly over to the kid, and Michael saw the same fury in his partner's eyes as he felt. God, vice sucked.

"Have them send the EMTs up as soon as things are under control down there. Every one of these boys needs to be taken to the hospital for evaluation."

"Roger that." His partner disappeared.

Michael turned to the boy, who lay shivering. "It's going to be okay." He holstered his gun and, pulling his jacket off, laid it over the kid.

He wanted to believe his own words, yet knew the sad truth was, things weren't okay for this boy or any of the others they'd found in this house of horrors. Maybe some of them would be able to go home. Not all of them had been kicked out for being gay or any other reason. Some of them had parents who were desperate for their son to be returned. No matter what, though, the recovery from this kind of abuse would take years, if not a lifetime.

In the meantime, this raid had netted some fish but not the big one. There was still someone out there running the ring that preyed on runaways and sold their bodies to as many men as they could find. Until Michael got the guy and brought him down, he'd be staring at a lot more terrified boys.

****

"Come on, give me bigger smiles."

Finn turned his lips up wider to please his uncle, Jack Malloy. He had his arms around his brothers, and their cousin, Regan Malloy, was on the other side of Ronan. All three of them were shiny in their uniforms, and he was proud to have them flank him.

Uncle Jack clicked a few times before lowering his camera. "That's fine, then. I'll have copies made big enough for framing."

"Wait, Dad, take a picture with my phone," Regan asked, holding it up to toss to her father.

Jack waved the notion away. "You know I can't deal with those things. I have what I need." So saying, he capped the camera lens and stuffed everything into the bag on his lap. Regan's father was confined to a wheelchair, thanks to a perp years back who'd pushed him down a flight of stairs. That didn't stop the guy from getting around, though, and Finn was touched he'd also shown up in his old uniform.

"Thank God," Daire said quietly. "I love you, little brother, but I hate having my picture taken." Daire slapped Finn on his back. "How about we head back home? Aunt Mary and the others have already left to get the food out."

Finn rolled his eyes. "Seriously, you don't have to go to so much trouble. It's not like I graduated high school or college." Even as he said it, he was secretly thrilled that so many of his family had come to graduation and were making such a fuss. He couldn't help looking down again at the metal pinned to his chest. He was so damned proud of being accepted onto the force. There was only one thing that would make this day better—two things, people.

He had to blink away the tears that sprang up all of a sudden. It was too much to hope his brother wouldn't notice.

Hugging him closer, Daire said into his ear, "They're here. I feel it."

Finn shot him a reassuring smile, although he wasn't so sure his brother was right. He'd tried so many times to detect the presence of his parents, had lain endlessly in his bed late at night trying to see, hear, or feel that some part of them remained. There had been nothing.

Still, he honored them as best he could with what he did with his life. Doing well in high school, getting into Boston College, the family alma mater, and now graduating from the Academy and joining the force—that was his way of keeping them close. And halfway through college, he'd also done the one thing he needed to do to be true to himself, the thing he couldn't do when they'd died. He'd come out.

"Come on," Ronan urged as he clamped his arms around Finn. "I'm starving. Let's go."

Before they could take a step toward the exit, the police commissioner strode up, his hand extended. All three of the Callaghan brothers stood up straight, and Finn took the proffered hand. Sean Finnegan was Finn's namesake and godfather and had been their father's best friend. It wasn't the same as having his actual father there, but it was a close second.

"Congratulations, Finn, my boy," the older man said, his big hand clasping Finn's firmly. "It's another proud day for the Callaghans and brought tears to my eyes to hear you speak of your father."

"Thank you, sir. I couldn't not mention him."

"Of course not. He was the finest man and best cop I knew. It makes no difference what some here might think. We know he was honorable."

"Yes, sir." Finn fought to keep the smile on his face. Although he couldn't see his brothers' expressions, he knew they were forcing themselves not to grimace. It was an infuriating fact that the rumors of his father being on the take and his parents being murdered in some kind of double cross of the so-called Irish mob wouldn't die. He knew both of his brothers hadn't given up trying to uncover the truth. He'd vowed to do the same now that he was a cop.

"Well, I'm sorry I won't be able to stop by for your party." The commissioner made a face. "I have to go to an event hosted by the mayor."

"I understand, sir. Thank you again for your good wishes."

Finnegan gave a wave and a nod to each of the brothers before striding off. Ronan made a rude noise under his breath.

"Political brownnoser."

"Ronan!" Daire admonished.

"It's true and you know it. He's never lifted a finger to clear Dad's name. Doesn't want any of the stink to rub off on him."

"Let it go," Daire ordered. "Today is Finn's day. We remember the happy and let the rest go for now."

"For now," Ronan agreed and, slapping Finn on his back, he said, "Food!"

Finn laughed because it was what his brothers wanted. But as he walked off with them, he silently agreed with Ronan. None of his father's friends on the force had wanted to look too hard at what had happened. They were afraid of either being painted by the same brush or of what they'd find. The Callaghan brothers weren't afraid of either thing. They knew their father hadn't been dirty, and they'd find the truth no matter where it led them.

****

Washington's sneeze was loud enough to envelop the lieutenant's tiny office. Michael stopped mid-sentence and glared at his partner.

"Sorry, man," Washington said through the wad of tissue up against his nose. "This damn cold keeps getting worse."

"Maybe it's allergies," Lieutenant Bates said. "They're wicked bad this time of year."

"Yeah, I don't think so, LT," Washington replied. "Feels like I've got a fever."

Michael blew out a frustrated breath. "Jesus

fucking Christ, can we get back to the raid?" His partner glared peevishly at him and nodded. "Anyway, LT, we've got the boys under the supervision of child protective services. We can't interview them until they've been medically cleared, then we need to make sure they have a lawyer present with a social worker or parents if we can get them here, and blah, blah, blah. Bottom line, we've got a bunch of traumatized minors and some low level pimps and enforcers from whom we've sweated as much information as we can, and we're still no closer to nailing the guy in charge than we were when we started."

"I thought your informer said the guy would be there."

Michael paced a circle in the small space. "That's what he said, and he's a reliable snitch. We found one room in that piece-of-crap house that didn't need to be fumigated. It was done up a little nicer than the other rooms and looked like it had been recently occupied, given the sheets were rumpled and warm. My guess is the asshole got tipped off and ran right before we got there."

"Leaving his people behind? Sounds stupid to me. Why aren't any of them rolling on him?"

Another loud sneeze from Washington startled Michael. He grimaced at his partner, who shrugged. The poor guy did look a little glassy-eyed and sweaty.

"Given that we've stumbled over more than one dead body in this investigation, I'm thinking they're too scared to give him up. And we certainly had our hands full with who we found, so if he had left recently, we didn't notice."

The lieutenant sighed and tipped his head back to

gaze at the ceiling. "Where exactly does this leave us?"

Michael took a second to marshal his thoughts. He'd been pondering his next move for hours. He thought he had an idea that would work. "I want to try sending someone in undercover."

"You mean have someone infiltrate the organization?"

"No, sir. It would take forever to get someone to a point of being trusted. This guy hasn't been successful by taking chances. I was thinking of getting someone in from the other end of the operation. According to the boys we've rescued, once a boy is considered to be 'broken,' if you will, cowed into submission and at least no longer fighting them, they may get sent to spend time with the top man. Apparently he likes to consume what he sells. He's picky, though. He takes only the best looking boys, and he never spends more than a night or two with one. Most of the time, he comes to them. Rumor has it, though, once in a while a boy is sent to him. We just haven't managed to find any of those boys or at least none that will admit to it."

"I'm not following you."

Michael licked his upper lip. "Have someone pose as a runaway and maneuver to get him recruited by one of the pimp's boys."

Bates stared at him for several seconds with eyebrows raised. "You're looking for a cop to pose as a teenage boy?"

"Yes, sir. We've done it before with high school drug stings. We just need someone who looks sixteen or so and attractive enough to catch his attention. This fucker preys on boys much younger, but some of them are close to twenty. As long as they look young enough to the johns, they keep them on the string."

Bates nodded. "Okay, I can see it. It's worth a try."

"Yeah, but there's one more thing, LT." A small knot of apprehension formed in Michael's stomach. This was the tricky part. He knew he was right, though. "We need to pick a rookie, someone not known to a lot of the detectives and uniforms."

Washington coughed hard, not as a commentary, however. It sounded like the cold had travelled to his lungs.

Michael looked at him and frowned. "Seriously, man, you need to go home or something."

"I'm fine," his partner said stubbornly.

"Why do you want a fresh face?" the lieutenant asked, then held up his hand. "Never mind, stupid question. You think someone in the department is on this pimp's payroll."

"Yes, sir, I do, and believe me, it pains me to say it."

"Crap," Bates muttered and heaved a big sigh. "I agree." He tapped a pen against the edge of his desk in obvious thought. "I think I've got the right guy. You know Sergeant Daire Callaghan?"

"By reputation, yes."

"Well, his youngest brother just graduated at the top of the Academy's class earlier today. I dropped by for the ceremony, because Daire and I were classmates. The kid, Finn, fits the bill perfectly. You'd swear he was seventeen, tops, and even a straight guy like me recognizes he's a looker."

Michael stiffened a fraction of a second at the mention of sexuality before relaxing again. He knew Bates didn't mean anything by it, even knowing

Michael's orientation. While Michael didn't exactly march in any parades, he wasn't completely in the closet, either.

"Sounds like our man," he said neutrally.

"I can't say he wouldn't be recognized after giving the graduating speech, but maybe if we let his hair grow a little and put him in the right clothes, even someone who had seen him might not recognize him."

"It's a risk we have to take. We have to use a cop for the role, and a rookie is our best bet."

"Okay, then, I'll call Daire and set up a meet between you and Finn. We'll do it at their house so no one sees it."

Standing up, Michael nodded. "Sounds good, LT. Thanks."

"Yes, sir, thanks," Washington added before bending over in a half sneeze, half cough.

"Jesus, Washington," the lieutenant said as he picked up the phone. "Caruso's right. Go home."

Also Read

Untamed Heat

by

Tarah Scott

http://amzn.com/B00NS3LY60

He thinks she's a high-priced call girl. She thinks he's a womanizer.

Liz Williams intends to put a stop to her daughter's affair with archeology professor, Anthony Hawkins. But she's unprepared for the sexy as hell, thirty-two year old Native American, who denies any involvement with her daughter and makes her pulse race.

Hawk is sure the beautiful brunette in the back of his class isn't there to hear his lecture. Mature, confident, and looking at him with those bedroom eyes, she's just his type. Too late he realizes she's trouble. And he's got more than his share of that.

But when a crooked land developer's threats include Liz, the protector in Hawk takes over and together they face danger and a night of untamed heat in the desert.

Thank you for purchasing this
publication of The Wild Rose Press, Inc.
If you enjoyed the story, we would appreciate
your letting others know by leaving a review.
For other wonderful stories, please visit our
on-line bookstore at www.wilderroses.com.

For questions or more
information contact us at
info@thewildrosepress.com.

The Wild Rose Press, Inc.
www.thewilderroses.com

Stay current with The Wild Rose Press, Inc.

Like us on Facebook
https://www.facebook.com/TheWildRosePress

And Follow us on Twitter
https://twitter.com/WildRosePress